The Little Vampire
Takes a Trip

When Mr and Mrs Peasbody announce a relaxing family holiday at a farm in Nether Bogsbottom in a week's time, Tony is filled with dread – what on earth can happen in such a dead-end place? But, after he persuades Rudolph Sackville-Bagg (alias "the Little Vampire") to come with him, he's sure that it will be the most exciting holiday of his life!

The vampire-day party at the Sackville-Bagg family vault, with its games like coffin racing, helps the following week to pass quickly. And suddenly, it's time for them to set off to the holiday house. There is only one problem – how will Tony and Rudolph get the Little Vampire's coffin to Bogsbottom ...?

This book is for all the little vampire's friends, and especially for Katja, who has now learned to read (and likes reading vampire stories best, of course) – and for Burghardt Bodenburg, whose brittle teeth are beginning to get a bit more pointed.

Angela Sommer-Bodenburg

The Little Vampire

TAKES A TRIP

ANGELA SOMMER-BODENBURG

Translated by Sarah Gibson

Illustrated by Amelia Glienke

Hippo Books
Scholastic Publications Ltd.
London

Scholastic Publications Ltd.,
10 Earlham Street, London WC2H 9LN

Scholastic Inc.,
730 Broadway, New York, NY 10003, USA

Scholastic Tab Publications Ltd.,
123 Newkirk Road, Richmond Hill,
Ontario, L4C 3G5, Canada

Ashton Scholastic Pty. Ltd.,
PO Box 579, Gosford, New South Wales,
Australia

Ashton Scholastic Ltd., 165 Marua Road,
Panmure, Auckland 6, New Zealand

First published in West Germany by
Rowohlt Taschenbuch Verlag, 1982
First published in the UK by Andersen Press, 1984

Published in paperback by Scholastic Publications Ltd., 1985

Original title *Der kleine Vampir verreist*

ISBN 0 590 70408 7

Made and printed by Cox & Wyman Ltd, Reading, Berks

Typeset in Palatino by V & M Graphics Ltd, Aylesbury, Bucks

Contents

1

Looking at the Map

It was a mild spring evening. The sweet smell of jasmine was in the air and the moon bathed the houses on the estate in a soft silver light. The big hand of the town hall clock had just reached twelve, and the clock began to strike: one, two …

The little vampire sat at the top of the chestnut tree and counted softly with the chimes: seven, eight, nine. Nine o'clock. Surely that was not too early to visit his friend Tony? Tony's parents were bound to have gone out, as they did almost every Saturday evening, either to the cinema or to friends.

And that was just as well! thought the little vampire, because it had meant that Tony had been able to come with him on many a nocturnal adventure. To the Vampire Ball for instance, where Tony had dressed up as a vampire and had danced with him so that the other vampires would not notice Tony was really a human being. How funny Tony had looked, forced to gaze lovingly at the vampire as he danced!

The little vampire giggled. He was gradually getting hot in his woolly tights and the two cloaks he was wearing, one of which was for Tony. He decided to fly to Tony's window and knock.

The curtains of Tony's room were closed,

but the little vampire found a chink through which he could peep into the room. He saw Tony sitting on the floor, hunched over a large map by the light of the lamp on his desk.

The vampire tapped on the window pane with his long fingernails and, cupping his hands round his mouth, called, "It's me, Rudolph!"

Tony lifted his head. His face looked startled for a moment, then cleared. He came over to the window and opened it.

"Hi," he said. "I thought for a moment it was Aunt Dorothy!"

The vampire laughed. "You don't need to worry about Aunt Dorothy today. She's gone to a barn dance," he said, as he clambered into the room.

"To dance?"

"'Course not. She's probably lurking by the hall waiting for the first guests to go home. And then ..." He burst into cackles of laughter and Tony caught a glimpse of his canine teeth: they were as sharp as needles. As usual, he went all goose-pimply. "Actually," continued the little vampire gleefully, "she can't stand those people. Last time they had had so much to drink that Aunt Dorothy lay in her coffin for two whole nights with alcohol poisoning!"

"Eeeugh!" said Tony softly. He preferred not to be reminded of the fact that vampires, including his best friend, live on blood. Luckily Rudolph was always full up by the time he came to visit Tony.

The little vampire pointed to the map.

"Homework?"

"No," said Tony darkly. "This afternoon I had to go and look over a farm with my parents. Here, in this god-forsaken hole!"

He pointed to a dot on the map and the vampire bent forward to read the name: "Nether Bogsbottom?"

"Yes, that's what the dump's called," answered Tony, "and that's where my parents want to go for a whole week's holiday!"

"On their own?"

"I've got to go with them, of course. For some real relaxation, as Dad puts it. Far from the city noise, to breathe in the country air, go for long walks -" At this, he sounded so disgusted that the vampire had to laugh.

"It won't be as bad as all that," he said.

"What do you know about it?" cried Tony, his face turning scarlet with annoyance. "There are just cattle, cackling hens and neighing horses as far as the eye can see! There's absolutely nothing to do at all!"

"What about riding?"

"Pooh, riding - on those carthorses!"

"Or going on a tractor?"

"Boring. I'd like to go on holiday where there are proper things to do. But in Nether Bogsbottom -" He ran his finger over the map in irritation. "Just listen to the names of the next door villages: Upper Bogsbottom, Bogs-bottom-in-the-Marsh, East Batsteeple, West Batsteeple. What on earth can ever happen in those dead-end places?"

He felt tears welling up and quickly wiped

his eyes so that the little vampire would not notice. His parents had planned a whole week's holiday there without even asking him! They had just found a farm in a deserted bit of country and expected him to be pleased about it! Ah, he would have known where to go! To a real "health" resort, for instance, one with a swimming pool, a whole heap of restaurants, cinemas, discos! But no one thought of him and what he'd like to do!

"I'd have thought it sounded very nice," broke in the vampire.

"I don't agree," said Tony grumpily. Then he gave a start. He had just had an idea. "Do you really think so?" he asked.

"Yes. I think the villages sound promising. As if there might be vampires there. Perhaps you'll get to know a couple if you go over to the cemetery in Bogsbottom-in-the-Marsh after dark."

"Me?" said Tony cryptically, and then added with a grin: "You mean, we!"

"We?"

"Yes," said Tony. "You can come too. If you were there, it'd be the most exciting holiday of my life."

"But –" The vampire was speechless.

"Didn't you just say you thought it sounded very nice?" challenged Tony.

"I meant for you."

"What's good enough for me is good enough for you. Or aren't we friends?"

"Of course we are, but –"

"And didn't I help you when you were

4

banished from the vault and left on the streets with your coffin? Didn't I hide you in our basement?"

"Yes, but –"

"Well then. Now you can do something for me."

The vampire turned away and began to chew his nails. "It's all so sudden," he muttered crossly. "We vampires don't like to be rushed into things."

"Who's talking about being rushed?" asked Tony. "My parents aren't leaving until next Sunday. We've got time to think it all out in peace. How we're going to get your coffin to Nether Bogsbottom, for instance."

The vampire gave a little start. "What if it gets lost on the way?" he cried. "That would be the end of me."

"Quite. That's why we must plan everything down to the last detail. Perhaps we could –"

At that moment, they heard voices at the front door.

"My parents!" hissed Tony in fright. "They don't usually come home so early."

The vampire had reached the window-sill in a single bound. He spread out his cloak.

"Come back tomorrow evening," Tony called after him. "We'll talk about it again."

2

Frail Nerves

Tony closed the window, drew the curtains and began to fold away the map. Any minute now, his mother would come in because she had noticed the light under his door.

"Are you still awake, Tony?" she called, tapping on the door.

"Hmmm," he mumbled.

His mother came in and looked at him in surprise. "You haven't even got undressed!"

"No."

"And it's so stuffy in here again ..." She strode swiftly over to the window and opened it wide. "You should always have some fresh air before you go to bed. A stuffy room isn't healthy."

"Okay, okay," said Tony, giggling to himself. She wasn't to know that it was traces of Rudolph that she could smell. "Why did you come back so early?"

"Had you got something planned?"

"No. I only wanted ..."

"To watch telly, I bet."

"Me? Watch telly? I've been looking at the map." As he had not yet managed to fold it up properly, he spread it out on the floor again. "I wanted to know what there was around Nether Bogsbottom."

"And what have you discovered?"

"West Batsteeple. That sounds pretty interesting. Perhaps there are vampires there."

"You and your vampires!" His mother immediately sounded cross. "You never think of anything else. That's what comes of reading all those vampire stories." She went to the bookcase and took out Tony's favourite books. *Dracula – The Revenge of Dracula – Vampires – Twelve Chilling Vampire Tales – In the House of Count Dracula – Voices from the Vault –* One after the other, she let the books drop onto the bed. "It makes me shivery just to read the titles."

Tony winced as each book landed on the bed. But he kept quiet so as not to provoke his mother any further, otherwise she might take the books right away.

"You just have frail nerves," was his only comment as he picked up the books and put them back carefully in the bookcase.

"And you haven't, I suppose? If only you could hear yourself moaning and groaning in your sleep sometimes."

"That just means I'm dreaming about school!"

"Oh really? Is there a Dorothy at school then?"

"Dorothy?" Tony went pale.

"Last night you called out: 'Aunt Dorothy, please don't bite me!' How do you explain that?"

"Well – that was –" He searched carefully for the right words. "That's the cleaning lady. She's got such pointed teeth. And just the other day I left my sports bag in the classroom by mistake, so I went back to fetch it – and there – and there she was, with her sharp pointed teeth, just looking at me ..." He had broken out into a sweat as he spoke, but his mother simply smiled, unconvinced.

"If I know you, you wouldn't move a muscle to fetch a sports bag."

"There was money in it," he said quickly. How was it that his mother always managed to catch him out? No matter what fantastic stories he thought up, she always saw straight through them. There was only one thing for it: to tell the truth!

"All right then!" He took a deep breath. "Aunt Dorothy is the aunt of Rudolph, the little vampire, of Anna the Toothless and of Gruesome Gregory. What's more, she's the most dangerous vampire in the Sackville-Bagg family!"

For one moment, his mother was too taken aback to answer. Then her eyes began to glow and she exploded. "I've had just about enough of these endless vampire stories!"

"Dad hasn't," remarked Tony.

"What do you mean?"

Tony nodded at the door. "He's just switched on the telly. There's a vampire film on: 'Dracula, the Lonely Wanderer'."

The sounds came softly through to them.

"You seem strangely well-informed," remarked his mother.

Tony felt himself turn red. Of course, he could not admit he had been looking forward to the film all evening.

"But then you would be."

"What?"

"You wanted to watch it yourself. If only we hadn't come home so early ..."

"But, Mum!" protested Tony.

"I know, I know," said his mother, "but this time you won't get away with it, because now you're going to get undressed instead and go to bed."

"Okay," muttered Tony, trying to look suitably disappointed. But he had to bite his lips to stop himself smiling. His mother had apparently forgotten that he had his own television set in his bedroom!

3

Bad Books

At breakfast the next morning, Tony's father asked: 'So you've decided you do want to come to the farm after all?"

"Mmmm," said Tony evasively.

"I can't understand why you didn't want to," declared Dad. He poured himself another cup of coffee and warmed to his subject. "It's the dream of every city boy: climbing trees, building tree-houses, having paperchases, going on night explorations –"

Tony looked up from his plate in surprise. "Is that what we're going to do? I thought you only wanted to go on ordinary walks."

His parents exchanged looks.

"Of course we want to go for walks," said Dad. "We want to get fit and healthy. And perhaps paperchases are a little too strenuous for us." He saw how Tony's face had fallen, so he added quickly: "But there are lots of different things for you to do on the farm. You can help with feeding the animals, and go out with the farmer. And there are children in the family, too. I think the boy is exactly your age.

"Tony is a year younger," said Mum.

"Oh, him!" said Tony with a dismissive gesture. "He's only interested in knights. He says he's got five hundred models in his room."

10

His father laughed. "Then you'll get on well together – him with his knights and you with your vampires."

Tony choked. It was monstrous to compare knights with vampires. "Knights died out hundreds of years ago!" he exclaimed. "Chivalry went out with the Middle Ages!"

"I suppose vampires still exist?" said his mother scornfully.

Tony quickly bent over his plate. "Of course not," he said, hiding a smile with difficulty. "Vampires only exist in books – in bad books, what's more," he added. "Isn't that right?"

How do vampires go on holiday? Tony spent the whole of Sunday wrestling with the problem, but instead of coming up with a solution, he could only think of more difficulties. The nub of the problem was that vampires always have to sleep in their own coffins. Therefore they can only travel if they take their coffin with them. But how? It wouldn't fit into a suitcase, and the vampire couldn't tuck it under his arm and fly with it.

What if we send it on ahead as luggage? wondered Tony. He had often read in the papers of people who died while they were on holiday, and were brought back to their home town in a coffin. But wouldn't the railway officials be a bit suspicious if he, Tony, were to give in a coffin as a piece of luggage?

Tony sighed. If only he had someone to discuss it with. But he had to keep it a secret from his parents, and the little vampire wouldn't want to be bothered with such problems. Tony's glance fell on his books. Surely there was a story about a vampire going on a journey which he could get an idea from? Of course: *Dracula* – the book by Bram Stoker! Count Dracula wanted to emigrate from Transylvania to England!

Tony took down the book from the shelf in excitement. It was a few months since he had read it, and he couldn't remember all the details, but he did know that fifty large chests played an important part in the Count's travelling preparations. The book began with an entry from the diary of Jonathan Harker, an English lawyer, who had invited Dracula to his castle.

"30th June, morning ..." read Tony. "The great box was in the same place, close against the wall, but the lid was laid on it, not fastened down, but with the nails ready in their places to be hammered home ... I raised the lid and laid it back against the wall ... There lay the Count, but looking as if his youth had been half-renewed ... the mouth was redder than ever, for on the lips were gouts of fresh blood ... As I write there is in the passage below a sound of many tramping feet and the crash of weights being set down heavily, doubtless, the boxes with their freight of earth. There is a sound of hammering, it is the box being nailed down ..."

The box ... that was Dracula's coffin. But why did he need the other ones? So it would

12

be difficult to discover him? If there were only one chest, someone might easily open it, but if there were fifty ...

Not a bad idea, mused Tony. Unfortunately, it was out of the question for Rudolph and himself, for they did not have the coaches to transport them, and they did not want to go by ship either.

Outside it was already getting dark. Tony's father came in, carrying a plate of sandwiches and a glass of milk.

"Mum thinks it's time you went to bed," he said, and put the plate down near Tony. He bent over inquisitively and tried to read the title of the book.

"Vampire stories?" he asked.

"I've got a problem to solve," announced Tony loftily and snapped the book shut. He put it down on his pillow and took a cheese sandwich. "Perhaps you can help."

"Me?"

"You work for a transport company, don't you?"

"Yes –"

"So you often have to send things."

His father smiled. "Of course."

"I have a friend," said Tony, "who wants to send something."

"Oh? What sort of thing?"

"A chest. About as long as this." Tony stretched out his arms. "Perhaps a little longer."

"Quite a size then," said his father. He did not seem to be taking Tony's question

13

seriously. "What's your friend got in this chest? Pearls? Gold? Jewels?"

Tony bit his lip. "I thought you were going to help me."

"I will, I will. But I must know what sort of cargo we're talking about." And with a glance at Tony's book, he added, "It might even be a vampire's coffin, mightn't it? We don't transport things like that. We're a reputable company."

At first Tony was afraid his father was suspicious, but now he realised he was only making fun of him. So there was no need to mince matters!

"What a shame!" he said nastily. "Actually it does happen to be a vampire's coffin!"

His father did not believe a word, of course. "In that case," he teased, "your friend should go to a firm of funeral directors!" He went over to the door. "Mum and I are going out for a stroll," he said.

"Will you be long?" asked Tony in surprise.

"Long enough for you to be asleep by the time we get back," answered his father. "You've got school tomorrow."

"As if I'd forgotten!"

4

Fragrant Dew

It's almost like clockwork! thought Tony as, shortly after his parents had left, something tapped gently on his window. He pulled the curtains happily to one side – and jumped.

There on the window-sill outside, someone was crouching looking at him with wide-open eyes, and although the figure was hidden in shadow and had pulled its cloak right up to its chin, Tony was sure it was not the little vampire. Was it Aunt Dorothy? An icy shudder ran through him and hastily he pulled the curtains to.

Then the tapping came again and a bright little voice called, "Hey, it's me, Anna!"

Rudolph's little sister! Relieved, but also somewhat annoyed, Tony opened the window and let her in. "Did you have to give me such a fright?" he grumbled.

Anna smoothed down her cloak and giggled. In the glow of his desk lamp, it seemed to him that her little round face was unusually rosy. Her hair was brushed and held back from her face with two slides.

"I only wanted to see if you knew any other vampire girls," she said teasingly. "If by chance you'd called: 'Hello, Julia!' I wouldn't have asked you to my vampire-day party."

"Vampire-day party?"

"Today's the day I became a vampire!" she

explained proudly. "My birthday, as it were. The only anniversary we vampires keep. Look what Rudolph gave me." She pulled a well-thumbed book out from under her cloak and showed it to him. "It's really exciting."

"I know," answered Tony, who recognised the book at once. It was *Monstrous Mouthfuls*, a book he had lent the little vampire a couple of weeks earlier.

"Why, have you read it?" asked Anna.

"No, no," he replied quickly, "it just looks exciting."

"And from Greg I got these hair slides," she said.

They did not look particularly new to Tony, but still, it was nice of Gregory to have given his sister a present.

"And I'm wearing my best present," she continued, "although you can't see it."

"Can't see it?" echoed Tony, puzzled.

"Just smell it!"

"Ah!" So he had not been mistaken in thinking there was a most extraordinary smell coming from Anna. "A new perfume?"

"Right!" she said. "Especially for me: Fragrant Dew!"

Tony gulped. The Fragrant Earth which Anna had used before was bad enough – but Fragrant Dew! It smelt of smelly cheese, sweaty feet and stink bombs!

"What else did you get?" he asked quickly, before she tried to find out what he thought of the perfume.

She hesitated, then an embarrassed smile

crossed her face. "I'll only tell you if you promise not to laugh."

She reached under her cloak and pulled out a rubber dummy. It was long and well-sucked, dirty white in colour and attached to a ring by what looked like a black shoelace. Tony had to bite his tongue in order not to laugh. Anna with a dummy! That was really too much!

She was studying him anxiously. When he remained straight-faced, in fact a little pained-looking because his tongue was hurting, she breathed a sigh of relief.

"It's for my teeth," she explained. "Every grown-up vampire has to have one so that our front teeth stay small and our canine teeth grow nice and long."

Tony was shocked. Up till now, she had been Anna the Toothless, and had fed only on milk.

"Will your canine teeth grow?" he asked.

"Maybe," she said evasively. "A little bit – but I'll only use my dummy when I'm in my coffin," she added quickly, "and only when I feel like it." With that, she hid it away under her cloak. "Now we should get going," she announced.

"Where to?"

"To the vault of course."

"The vault?" Tony was taken aback. "What for?"

"To my vampire-day party!" said Anna cheerily.

Tony noticed how his heart began to beat faster. Birthday parties he knew about, they were fun. But vampire-day parties ...? They

17

were bound to be gruesome. Perhaps Anna had already grown vampire teeth and wanted to try them out on him in the vault! He began to feel very odd, and had to steady himself at the desk.

"I-I don't think I can," he stuttered, "I have to wait here for Rudolph."

"But he's at the vault of course!" She threw a second cloak over him which she had kept hidden under her own.

"Come on!" she said. "Otherwise Greg will be getting impatient."

"Gregory will be there too then?"

"Of course," answered Anna. "He loves vampire-day parties."

"Wh-what about your other re-relations?" asked Tony. "Aunt Dorothy, and William the Wild and Thelma the Thirsty and Sabina the Sinister and Frederick the Frightful?"

"They're all out on business."

There was a pause. Tony gazed helplessly at the moth-eaten, musty-smelling cloak in his hands, as Anna climbed up on the window-sill. Should he really go with her? At least he'd meet Rudolph there, because he certainly would not come to Tony on his sister's vampire-day, even though they had arranged it. And there wasn't much time left before next Sunday ...

"Okay," he agreed in a hollow voice. He slipped the cloak on and climbed up to the window-sill with Anna. She looked at him and smiled. Then she spread her arms and sailed away.

Shakily, Tony followed her.

5

In the Air

As usual when he wore a vampire cloak and was able to fly, Tony had a funny feeling in his tummy. He pumped his arms unsteadily up and down and squinted down anxiously at the cars which looked like toys, six storeys below him. Then he felt the air supporting him. His movements grew stronger, his gliding steadier. It was like swimming, only much smoother and needed less effort.

"You fly like a real vampire!" Anna congratulated him as she flew alongside.

"Really?" he said, with an embarrassed grin.

Although she had meant it kindly, he felt uneasy at her words. Was he about to turn into a vampire? On the other hand, he knew very well that a human could only be changed into a vampire by a bite from one of them. His fear that Anna might try out her new teeth on him once they were in the vault began to well up again, and he watched her narrowly from the corner of his eye. She looked really strange in the moonlight. Her face glimmered like a white flower beneath her dark hair. Her lips were half open and he could see her teeth, small and round like pearls. If she were really growing pointed teeth, he could not see them. Perhaps he was only imagining it.

"Watch out!" Anna pulled him out of his reverie. He nearly had not seen the chimney jutting up in front of him. At the last minute, he managed to dodge around it.

"You must look where you're going," scolded Anna. "The air is full of dangers. Look, there's Aunt Dorothy down there!"

"Wh-what?" stammered Tony. In his fright, he forgot to move his arms. Anna held him tightly by the cloak before he could drop to the ground.

"She's going to a Fire Brigade Ball," Anna reassured him. "That's what she told me."

He breathed a sign of relief. At least he did not have to worry that Aunt Dorothy might turn up unexpectedly at the vault while they were in the middle of celebrating Anna's vampire-day!

Before them lay the crumbling old wall of the cemetery. It ran round the deserted rear part of the graveyard, where the crosses and gravestones lay lopsided in the knee-high grass, seldom disturbed by any visitor. It was here that the vampire family of Sackville-Bagg had built their family vault, so as to be safe from the ambushes of the nightwatchman, Mr McRookery.

Anna flew slowly down the wall, gazing searchingly into the darkness. Tony, following at a little distance, whispered, "Can you see McRookery?"

She shook her head. "I expect he's sitting at home sharpening his wooden stakes," she said bitterly.

They crossed the wall and landed in front of a' tall yew tree. Anna quickly lifted a mossy

stone which lay in the shadow of the tree. It
was the entrance to the vault.

"Come on," she whispered, and disappeared
down the narrow shaft. Tony slid down after
her and pulled the stone back over the hole.

6

Lazybones

The smell of decay and Fragrant Dew that hit them was so strong that it almost took Tony's breath away. Trembling at the knees, he groped his way down the steps behind Anna, his heart in his mouth. Why on earth had he been so stupid as to come? There would surely have been another opportunity to talk to Rudolph. Down here, he was being handed over to Gregory – to Gregory and all the other vampires, who might come back at any moment ... or perhaps they were already waiting for him?

But in the candlelight, he could only see Gregory and Rudolph, lying in their coffins. The other coffins were shut. Tony breathed a sigh of relief. So it was true that the rest of the family were out hunting. Even so, he thought it would be wise to go carefully, so he waited on the bottom step where it was most in shadow.

Anna ran to the two open coffins and called excitedly: "You two lazybones! I thought you promised to get everything ready for my party!"

Rudolph sat up in his coffin and pulled a remorseful face. "My book was *so* exciting," he explained.

"What about Greg?"

"He fell asleep."

"And my party? I thought you were going to put the coffins together and decorate the vault."

"We were," said Rudolph in a subdued voice. "We did start to do it."

"Well?"

"Then Greg felt faint and had to lie down."

"His usual trick," scoffed Anna. "What will Tony think of us now?"

"Tony?" Rudolph sounded surprised. "Is he here then?"

"Y-yes," stammered Tony, stepping hesitantly out into the vault. "B-but I can go home again straight away," he added. "Don't put yourself out for me."

"That would be just great!" Anna said furiously. "No. You're staying here. If you're invited, you're invited. We must wake Greg up."

"Wake him up?" Rudolph looked worried. "You know what he's like when he's disturbed."

"I'm already awake," grunted a gravelly voice, and Gregory's ashen face rose out of his coffin. "Because of all the row you lot are making." His eyes were half-closed. "You've obviously never heard of consideration for others," he hissed.

Rudolph hurried over to help him up. "It's only because it's Anna's vampire-day," he soothed, "and because of Tony."

"Tony?" Gregory was suddenly wide awake. His penetrating gaze fell on Tony, who shivered.

"How could I have forgotten?" he said, and his voice became quite friendly. "Our visitor!" Smiling broadly, he advanced on Tony, took hold of him and growled: "You're heartily welcome!"

Tony turned white as a sheet. Heartily – that could only mean one thing: blood!

7

The Claws of a Beast of Prey

However, escape was out of the question: Gregory was much bigger and stronger than he was, and his hands held Tony as tight as a vice.

From that close, Tony studied the details of Gregory's face: the white skin, the red spots on his chin and on the end of his nose, the dangerous, smouldering eyes with their dark shadows and the wide mouth with its spotlessly white, jutting canine teeth. And he could smell Gregory's deathly breath: it was worse than Fragrant Dew!

He was about to pass out, he could feel it – but suddenly Anna was there, tugging at Gregory's cloak and saying, "If you're so pleased that Tony's here, you should prove it and get the vault arranged for him."

"Arrange the vault?" said Gregory sullenly. "That sounds too much like hard work." He gazed fixedly at Tony.

"Slacker," mouthed Anna, but luckily so quietly Gregory did not hear her.

"That's a nice sweater you've got there," he said to Tony. "Pure wool, isn't it?"

"I – er – don't know," stammered Tony, taking a step backwards.

Gregory held fast onto his sweater as if he were testing the material. "Or is it synthetic? Let me guess: I'd say 40% wool, 60%

synthetic. Am I right?" With a hefty jerk, he pulled Tony right up to him, rolled down the neck of the sweater and bared Tony's neck. As if through a mist, Tony saw Gregory's head coming nearer, bending over his own neck ...

He let out a terrified cry.

At once Gregory dropped his hands. "What's up with you?" he growled. "I only wanted to look at the label in your sweater." With heavy tread, he stomped over to his coffin and sat on the edge. "Anyway, I was right," he said. "40% wool, 60% synthetic."

With that, he pulled a nail file out from under his pillow and began to file the long curving nails of his left hand. The sight of these claws of a beast of prey was enough to make Tony's hair stand on end.

Gregory seemed absorbed in his occupation. A rapt smile was on his lips, and again and again he broke off to admire his nails, now more pointed than ever. "There's nothing to stop you starting," he remarked gently. He was so engrossed in what he was doing that he did not even lift his head.

"What with?" asked Anna.

"Arranging the room."

"But –" Anna started to protest, but Rudolph threw her a warning look and shook his head vigorously. He quickly went over to the five coffins standing against the left wall and began to push them around to form a seating area. Grinding her teeth, Anna joined in too.

"Sh-shall I help?" offered Tony.

"Not you," replied Anna, "but –"

"Yes?" interrupted Gregory. "Who?"

"Me of course," said Tony tactfully. Anything not to provoke Gregory, he thought. He went over to the foot of the last coffin, which must have been very heavy because Anna and Rudolph were having great difficulty in moving it. He noticed with a start that it was Aunt Dorothy's coffin ... suppose she was still in it?

Anna noticed his hesitation, and said gently, "The family heirlooms are in here. Aunt Dorothy guards them like a hen guards her chicks. Before she flies off, she always puts the treasure chest in her coffin."

"And it's this heavy?"

"Oh yes. It's solid gold."

"Do vampires wear jewellery?"

"If they want to look attractive to somebody. Also we need the treasure for funds. In hard times, we exchange some of it for cash. Vampires can't hold a bank account, of course."

"Hey, what are you whispering about over there?" It was Gregory's grating voice. "I bet you're talking about me!"

"No, no," said Anna quickly. "About where we are going to sit. We've made two coffins into a table and the other three are benches. Is that okay?"

"Only three as benches? There are four of us though." Gregory paused. Then he said cheerfully, "Never mind. Tony and I can share a coffin!"

"Oh no!" Tony could not stop himself.

"Why not?" asked Gregory. He had put the nail file back in his coffin and stood up. "Perhaps we'll play a guessing game. Then I'll be able to help you."

"I – I'd rather sit next to Anna," stuttered Tony. "I-It is her vampire-day, after all."

"As you like." Gregory sounded annoyed. He turned and climbed back into his coffin. "I hadn't finished filing my nails anyway."

Once more, the harsh grating of the nail file could be heard.

"So much the better," said Anna bitingly. "At least now everyone has a coffin to themselves. Come on, Tony!"

8

Food and Drink

Anna laid a hand on his arm and led him to the seats.

"Now, let's make ourselves cosy," she said happily – as if it were possible to be cosy here, twelve feet underground and in the company of the unpredictable Gregory! With beating heart, Tony sat down on the coffin nearest the way out, and Anna took her place beside him.

"You must be thirsty," she said. "As far as I know, there's always lots to eat and drink at birthday parties."

"Mmm," agreed Tony.

"You see?" she called over to Rudolph. He was leaning against the wall, reading his book, and he let it drop in vexation.

"How lucky it is that I have got something to drink," said Anna. "Could you bring it over, Rudolph?"

"Drink?" stuttered Tony. What on earth would there be to drink at a vampire-day party? With a shudder he pictured glass bottles full to the brim with blood! But in fact what Rudolph put down on the coffin-table were twenty or more tiny cartons of milk and chocolate milkshake. Packed in three somewhat dusty packets, they had been lying at the foot of Anna's coffin.

"Now, what about those?" said Anna proudly.

Tony stared speechlessly at the little cartons. There were almost enough to make a small dairy!

"I –" he mumbled. "I'm not thirsty," was what he wanted to say, but he kept silent so as not to annoy Anna. Now she was pulling out a rather crushed straw from the packet; she stuck it in the top of one of the chocolate cartons, and cheerfully offered the carton to Tony.

"Try it!"

"Th-thanks."

Reluctantly he took the carton which, in spite of the label saying "Choco-Drink is always fresh and tasty!" did not look in the least appetising; on the contrary, a thin layer of dust lay on the surface, and the corners were dogeared.

"What about you?" he asked. "Aren't you having any?"

Anna and Rudolph exchanged glances and giggled.

"Anna doesn't drink milk any more," explained Rudolph.

"No milk?" asked Tony. "But –"

"No chocolate milkshake either," continued Rudolph.

"Then who are all these cartons for?"

"For you," announced Anna.

"All of them?"

"Of course," she replied smiling rather embarrassedly. "They were for me originally, but now –" She did not go on, but quickly turned her head away. Tony saw she had blushed a deep red. Then he remembered the dummy, and how she had to have it in order to grow long canine teeth. She really had become – a vampire!

He felt the carton of chocolate milk in his hand tremble. The vampires noticed it as well. Suddenly they all seemed to be staring at him. Even Gregory had stopped filing his nails.

"Why don't you try it?" he called, his voice sounding menacing.

"I-I will," stammered Tony and sucked hard on the straw. He almost spat it out again – it tasted so revolting, like soap. Then he noticed the vampires were looking at him expectantly.

"V-very n-nice," he stammered.

"Well," growled Gregory, "they did taste even better."

"Anna's been keeping them for you," added Rudolph.

Anna smiled self-consciously.

"I don't need them any more." Then to Tony she said, "When you've finished, let me know, okay? I'll pass you another carton."

Tony nodded weakly. The thought of having to drink his way through another of the revolting things made him feel quite ill, but he knew how to get out of it: he would just pretend to drink it, so that one carton would last the whole evening.

Anna stood up, smoothed down her cloak and pushed the hair out of her eyes. "Now," she announced, "now we've finished eating and drinking, the best bit of the evening is about to begin!"

9

Coffin Racing

"Oh yes!" cried Gregory eagerly, clambering out of his coffin. "What shall we start with?"

"Yes, what shall we start with?" Anna turned to Tony and asked him. "What do you play at birthday parties?" Tony hesitated. In the present circumstances, any harmless game could well become mortally dangerous when played in a vault with vampires. On no account must he choose a game which needed the candles to be blown out – there was no knowing what Gregory might try out in the darkness! Nor any game that required hiding – then there would be the chance that Tony would have to crawl into a coffin!

"What about a sack race?" he suggested finally.

"Sack race?" Anna wrinkled her nose. "Sounds boring."

"I think so too," agreed Rudolph. "In any case, we haven't any sacks."

"Wait a moment!" said Gregory. "I've got an idea! What about coffin racing?"

"Coffin racing?" Anna still sounded dubious.

"Yes! We'll put several coffins in a row one behind the other, then you have to jump from coffin to coffin without falling in between. Whoever manages it is the winner."

"Is that all?" said Anna sullenly.

"Just wait and see."

Gregory put the lids on Rudolph's coffin and his own. Then he began to build the obstacle course. First came his own coffin, its only motif a "G" around which wound a two-headed dragon. Then came Rudolph's and Anna's coffins: neither had any decoration and they were much smaller than Gregory's. At the end of the course he put a large coffin with golden handles at the side. Tony seemed to remember it belonged to Thelma the Thirsty, the vampires' mother. The first two coffins were fairly close together, Tony thought, but the distance between the second and third was bigger and it seemed miles between Anna's and Thelma's coffins.

"I'll never do that," he murmured.

"It doesn't matter if you don't win," hissed Gregory nastily. He produced a box of matches from under his cloak, took out three and broke a length off each. Then he put the pieces between the fingers of his left hand so that they all looked the same length.

"You choose first," he said, nodding at Tony. When everyone – except Gregory – had taken one, they compared the length of their matchsticks: Rudolph had the shortest so he went first.

He managed to leap from the first to the second coffin easily. But even on his second jump, he got caught up in his cloak and fell to the ground. He got up slowly and tried the last jump, but did not make it. He fell against the side of Thelma's coffin. Dragging his right leg behind him and even paler than usual, he limped back to the others.

"One point," announced Gregory.

It was Tony's turn next. He hopped from Gregory's to Rudolph's coffin without difficulty. The gap from there to Anna's was wider, but he managed it.

"Bravo Tony!" shouted Anna.

"Ssssh!" said Gregory darkly. "No spectator encouragement!"

Just one more coffin to go … Tony held his breath and jumped. His knee bumped against the wood. "Ouch!" he cried. Wincing with pain, he limped back to the start.

"Two points," said Gregory.

Now it was Anna's turn. Her cloak was much too long, reaching down almost to her ankles, and it made her look fragile and tiny. Tony felt his heart beat faster.

Now she jumped, light-footed as a feather. She had already managed the first two. "Look out!" Tony wanted to call, but she had leaped through the air and landed on the last coffin – and then slid off again.

"Bad luck," was all Gregory said. "Two points, like Tony."

Head held high, Anna came back to them. "But I *am* the littlest!" she said proudly.

In the meantime, Gregory climbed onto his coffin and did a few knee-bends to limber up. Compared to Anna, he was tall and powerful, with broad shoulders and strong, muscular calves. No wonder he found it child's play to hop from coffin to coffin. When he reached

the last one, he threw his arms in the air and crowed.

"Greg, the greatest coffin racer of all time!"

"Clever Dick," growled Anna.

"Did you say something?" asked Gregory

affably. His eyes looked as dangerous as ever.

"No, no," said Anna quickly.

"Aren't I?" Gregory stood up straight and breathed deeply. "It's all due to my diet and way of life ..." He stared hard at Tony's neck and involuntarily bared his terrible teeth.

"Hey! That's enough, Greg!" cried Anna.

Gregory came to himself. Reluctantly, he tore his eyes away. "Enough of what?" he said grumpily.

10

Squeak, Piggy, Squeak!

"I know a game," said the little vampire.

"You do?" said Gregory in disbelief.

"Yes."

"What is it?"

"Squeak, piggy, squeak."

"Eeeek, eeeek!" Gregory tapped his forehead. "You've made it up."

"No I haven't," protested Rudolph. "There really is such a game."

"How do you know?"

"Well –" Rudolph put on a serious face and cleared his throat. "The children sat in a circle –"

"What children?"

"The children in the room that looked so warm and cosy from outside. I was frozen stiff and hungry, so I sat on the window-sill and watched them. One of them stood in the middle of the circle, blindfolded. He turned round and went and sat on another kid's lap. 'Squeak, piggy, squeak!' he said, and the second one squeaked. Then the one who was blindfolded had to guess whose lap he was sitting on."

Gregory seemed to like the sound of that game, because a smile began to spread over his face. "Doesn't sound so bad, your 'squeak, piggy, squeak'!" he said, "but bags I go in the middle!"

He groped under his cloak and pulled out a black cloth. It was full of moth holes.

"B-but you can see through that!" murmured Tony.

"So what?" hissed Gregory. "Do you want me to trip up?"

"N-no – it's just the rules of the game –"

"Pooh, rules!" said Gregory, and dismissed all further objection with a wave of his hand. "Just get me blindfolded!"

"Right," said Rudolph. He climbed onto a coffin and knotted the cloth behind Gregory's head.

"Shall we begin?" growled Gregory.

"Let's." Rudolph managed to push the two coffins which had served as a table back against the wall with some difficulty. Anna stood and watched and smiled scornfully.

"You're letting yourself be bossed around," she commented.

"What do you mean?" retorted Gregory. "He was the one who suggested this game."

His voice sounded muffled and ghoulish through the cloth. Rudolph gestured wildly to Anna not to argue with Gregory, but she appeared not to understand.

"You could easily have helped shift those," she said to Gregory. "You're by far the strongest."

"I know," said Gregory haughtily. "But that's no reason for you to lumber me with all the work. In any case, if you go on at me any more, I'll tell Aunt Dorothy that Tony was here."

"What!" exclaimed Tony. He looked at Anna in horror, but she gave a slight shake of her head.

"It's all just threats," she whispered.

Pleased with the effect his words had had, Gregory took a couple of tentative steps. "Where have you all gone?" he asked.

Anna and Tony quickly sat down on Aunt Dorothy's coffin. Rudolph took his place on the middle coffin.

"Ready!" he called.

Slowly Gregory came nearer. He was a fearful sight: instead of a face, all that was visible under the matted mane of hair was the moth-eaten cloth, and his powerful hairy forearms stuck out of the full cloak. He held his hands out in front of him and waved his long bony fingers searchingly backwards and forwards, as if finding it difficult to grope his way about. But Anna, Rudolph and Tony knew very well he could see them all quite clearly through the holes in the cloth!

At first, it looked as if he would sit on Rudolph's lap. Tony was just breathing a sigh of relief when Gregory took a couple of steps past Rudolph and stopped in front of him. Then he turned round and perched on Tony's lap. Tony thought he would suffocate, Gregory was so heavy and smelt so strongly of mould and decay.

"Squeak, piggy, squeak!"

"Eeeek!"

"Louder!"

"Eeeeeeeek!" squealed Tony.

"It's Tony!" cried Gregory, tore the cloth from his face and looked round triumphantly. "Have I won a prize?"

"No. But you are allowed to blindfold Tony," said Rudolph.

"Is that all?" grumbled Gregory. Crossly, he put the cloth round Tony's head and began to knot it. Suddenly he gave a shout. It was such a bloodcurdling cry that it made Tony's flesh creep.

"My fingernail!" he moaned. "It's broken!" He stared helplessly at the index finger of his left hand. "My best, my longest nail, tended and cared for, week after week! I was so proud of it – and now look!" he sobbed. Then he glared at Tony. "And it's all because of you!"

"M-me?"

"It was your head!" growled the vampire. "Your skull, your egghead, your nut, your stupid, stupid bonce!"

He rushed over to his coffin, found the nail and began to file the broken nail like a mad thing.

"It was your own fault," said Anna, "because you can't tie knots!"

"I *beg* your pardon?" thundered Gregory. "Is that all the thanks I get for staying behind in the vault for so long? Just to give you a nice vampire-day party? Well, that's the final straw!"

Snorting with rage, he flung the nail file back in his coffin and stomped off to the entrance to the vault.

"Big brothers should be banned!" shouted Anna after him. But Gregory did not answer. They heard the scrape of the stone – then all was quiet.

11

Rules Are Rules

"Now he's gone and spoilt everything," snivelled Anna.

"Why do you always have to fight with him?" asked the little vampire.

"Why?" cried Anna. "Because I can't stand being bossed around, that's why!"

"We three could go on with the party," suggested Tony timidly, trying to placate the pair of them. And without Gregory, it really might be fun ...

But Anna shook her head decisively. "No!" She pulled the slides from her hair and stuck them crossly under her cloak. "I'd rather go to the cinema!"

"To the cinema?" said Tony in surprise. "But the film will already have started and they won't let children in just like that!"

"Then what about a disco?"

"But –" began Tony. He wanted to say, "They won't let us in there either," but this would have made Anna even more angry. Instead he said, "I haven't got any money."

"Money? No problem." She went over to Aunt Dorothy's coffin and lifted off the lid to reveal a worm-eaten old chest. Anna opened it and took out two gold pieces. They gleamed and twinkled in the candlelight, almost taking Tony's breath away.

"Is that enough?" she asked.

But before Tony could reply, Rudolph came over, and took the gold pieces from Anna.

"That's against the rules!" he roared. "The gold pieces are to be kept for emergencies!"

"Isn't this an emergency?" cried Anna. "First you go and spoil my vampire-day party, and when I want to go to the disco just to have a bit of fun on my vampire-day, you won't even let me have two measly gold pieces!"

"Rules are rules!" retorted Rudolph. He put the money back in the chest and shut it carefully. Then he pushed the lid back on Aunt Dorothy's coffin. Anna shook her fist at him angrily.

"You – you *camel!*"

Rudolph grinned. "Camel? How sweet!"

"You stupid oaf, you brute!" Tears spurted from her eyes. Unexpectedly, she spun round and ran to the entrance. "I've had enough. I'm going!" she said.

"Anna!" called Tony, horrified.

"Rudolph can take you home," she sobbed – then she was gone.

12

It's Different for Vampires

A chilly gust of air streamed into the vault, making the candles flicker. Tony shivered. It occurred to him that his parents had only gone out for a walk. Suppose they had come home long since and noticed he wasn't in bed?

"Y-you will take me home, won't you?" he asked anxiously.

"Just wait a minute," replied the little vampire. He went to his coffin, took off the lid and lay down. "I need a little rest after that exhausting party," he said.

"But I must go home *now!*" protested Tony.

The vampire yawned. "You can't be in that much of a hurry." He took out his book and thumbed through it till he found his place. "The story about Mrs Lunt is so exciting," he said warmly. "I'm just at the bit where the man sits down in the armchair and begins to smell the stink –" He giggled. "Do you know what it is that stinks?"

Of course Tony did know the story, one of the *Vampire Stories* by Hugh Walpole. The smell was Mrs Lunt, who had been dead for a year. All the same, he shook his head.

"I've forgotten," he said.

"I never forget what I've read," boasted the vampire.

"You just forget to give back the books!"

"What? Which ones?"

"*Monstrous Mouthfuls!*" You gave it to Anna, even though it belongs to me!"

"I only lent it to her."

"Anna said you gave it to her as a vampire-day present."

"So what? Tomorrow her vampire-day will be over and I can get it back."

"But if you *gave* it to her –"

"It's different among us vampires."

"Well, that's charming," said Tony. Even at the risk of making Rudolph angry, he just could not keep quiet about something so unfair! But the vampire simply smoothed over the page, looking bored. "Can't you let me read in peace?" he growled.

"Now wait a moment," said Tony, raising his voice. Now he would find out if the vampire was a real friend or not! "We must talk about our holiday."

The vampire's expression altered at once. His grumpy look disappeared and he began to smile. "What about it? Isn't it all arranged?"

"What do you mean?" asked Tony.

"I mean I've decided to come with you."

For a second, Tony was speechless. Then he yelled: "You're really coming too? Oh Rudolph!" He was so overcome that he spread wide his arms and ran over to the vampire. "You're a real friend!"

"Aren't I?" smiled the vampire, looking pleased with himself. "Unlike Greg, who's invited George to stay in the vault."

"George who?"

"George the Boisterous. The one who won

the Perfume Prize at the Vampire Ball."

"Oh, him." Tony could remember the bald-headed, thickset vampire well, who had paraded around the stage, puffed up and conceited, and had allowed himself to be sniffed by all the judges.

"Didn't he win a blanket for his coffin?" he asked.

"That's right," said the little vampire between clenched teeth. He went to Gregory's coffin and pulled out a black woollen cloth. "But he gave it to Greg because apparently his feet are always cold."

"*Gave* it to him?" grinned Tony. "Lent it, I suppose. Things are different among …"

But Rudolph did not notice the sarcasm. A grim look on his face, he pulled out of Gregory's coffin a watch chain, a cigarette case, a tie pin with pearls and a pocket comb. "Here. All this came from George the Boisterous. So in return, Greg has invited him to stay at the vault. For a whole week from Saturday night. Even though I told him that on absolutely no account must I cross paths with George the Boisterous."

"Why not?" asked Tony.

"Because he might recognise me."

Tony shook his head. He was still in the dark. "Why mustn't he recognise you?"

"It was six weeks ago," began the little vampire. "I was flying back to the cemetery when I noticed a young man, certainly very juicy, walking along the street. I hadn't eaten much, so I landed a couple of feet behind him and began to stalk him. Then suddenly there was a loud noise from the bushes nearby. It was George the Boisterous, who had been lying there in wait and who now thought I was going to pinch his prey. He rushed towards me in a rage. I ran off, followed by George. Before he could catch me, he slipped on a dog's mess and fell flat on his face! I quickly squeezed through a hole in the hedge, but I could hear George thundering behind me: 'One of these nights I'll get you! Then I'll

pulverise you!'" The little vampire stopped, and stared morosely in front of him.

Tony had to bite his lip so as not to make his delight too obvious. He had expected so many things – Rudolph's usual casual attitude, his endless sighs and complaints, a hundred excuses – but not that he would be so ready to come on the holiday. And not only that: fear of George the Boisterous would make sure he did not change his mind, because he would have had to hide away somewhere in any case. Now there was just the problem of how to get the vampire with his coffin to Nether Bogsbottom.

But the vampire seemed to have thought of that. "We'd better go by train," he said. "You can bring me something to wear and then we can travel as two normal people. I've always wanted to sit in a train, not just fly over them."

"What about your coffin?"

"We'll pack it up. In wrapping paper!" The vampire giggled.

"How do you know if there is a train to Nether Bogsbottom?" asked Tony.

"Might there not be?" cried the vampire.

"Perhaps the railway doesn't go to such a dump," said Tony.

The vampire looked crestfallen. "I hadn't thought of that," he murmured. Then his eyes lit up again. "We'll go as near as we can. In any case, you'll have to find out about train times and connections."

"Me?" said Tony. "Us, you mean. It's you

who wants to get to Nether Bogsbottom."

"Okay, but no one will tell a vampire that sort of thing," said Rudolph softly.

"Then let's both go to the station!" announced Tony.

13

Ghosts in Tony's Room

Half an hour later, Tony and the little vampire landed in the top of the great chestnut tree in front of Tony's flat.

"Your window's open," whispered the little vampire, who could see much better than Tony in the dark.

"I hope my parents aren't back yet," murmured Tony.

At that moment, the front door of the block opened and Tony recognised Mrs Starling, leading her fat little dachshund, Susie, on a lead. Susie stopped dead, lifted her nose and sniffed. Then she began to yap.

"Ssssh!" hissed Mrs Starling.

But Susie barked even more loudly and strained at her lead: she wanted to get to the chestnut tree! The little vampire stirred uneasily on his branch. "I think I'd better fly," he grunted, then added urgently: "Don't forget! Saturday at the old cemetery wall. And bring some of your gear with you!"

"And you bring your coffin!" replied Tony.

The little vampire spread wide his cloak and glided away.

Mrs Starling threw an anxious glance up at the windows of the flats, then she pulled Susie over to the bushes round the play-ground. When she had gone, Tony flew to his room and shut the window behind him. He could see a light under his bedroom door. Were his parents back? Or had they forgotten to switch the light off?

Hurriedly, he pulled the vampire cloak over his head and hid it in the cupboard, under the old Austrian leather breeches, which he never wore, and the jerkin that went with them which his grandmother had knitted for him. Then he listened. Wasn't that his mother's voice he could hear from the kitchen? He opened the door a crack and was able to hear what was being said.

"And I'm telling you, he's not in his bed!" His mother sounded worried.

"Then he's on the loo," replied his father.

"No he isn't. I've looked there."

"Then he must have crept into your bed."

"No – he isn't in our room either."

"Then you can't have looked properly."

"Not looked properly?" exclaimed his mother. "Go and check for yourself!"

"Okay, I will."

Tony heard his father push back his chair and stand up. With a bound, Tony was in bed with the covers pulled up to his chin. Almost immediately, he heard his door open.

"Well, look at that." It was his father whispering. "He's fast asleep!"

His mother came into the room and stood by his bed. Although Tony had his eyes tightly closed, he felt her examining him from head to toe. But his shoes, jeans and jumper were well hidden!

"Funny –" She hesitated. "I could have sworn his bed was empty."

"It's easy to make a mistake."

"But the window – it was open a moment ago!"

"You're imagining things!"

Tony had to bite his tongue in order not to laugh. His mother was much more astute than his father. Luckily for him, in the face of his father's supposedly wider experience of the world and human nature, his mother was not usually allowed the courage of her convictions and so far had not caught Tony out. This seemed to be the case again this time, because she went to the door and shut it quietly behind her.

But out in the hall she said suddenly: "His clothes weren't there!"

Tony's heart nearly stopped. It didn't bear thinking about, what would happen if they came back and found he was fully dressed in bed …

But his father just laughed. "You're overworked, Hilary! You're seeing ghosts!"

"If you say so," she said, sounding hurt.

Their steps died away. Then came the sound of the television.

Much relieved, Tony got up, switched on his desk lamp and undressed. He put his shoes together in front of his bed and hung his jumper and trousers over a chair. He was not normally so tidy, but Mum might look in again, he thought with a grin.

He put on his pyjamas, switched off the light and snuggled back into bed. Now he could think over what the man at the railway station had said in peace.

14

At the Station

Leaving the little vampire hidden beneath a fir tree outside the station, which luckily was empty, Tony had gone over to the ticket office.

"Well, young man?" asked the man behind the counter.

"I'd like some information," announced Tony in a loud voice, swallowing his disgust at the "young man" bit.

"What would you like to know?"

"What time on Saturday is there a train to Nether Bogsbottom?"

"I must look it up. Morning or afternoon?"

"Evening. Around nine."

The man opened a directory and thumbed through it. "What was the place again?"

"Nether Bogsbottom."

He shook his head. "No train there," he said.

"Isn't there?" Tony went white. "But I've got to get there."

"Perhaps you could get out at the next door village. Do you know what that's called?"

"Upper Bogsbottom."

The man consulted his book again. Finally he closed it with a smile and said cheerfully, "There you are! Upper Bogsbottom. Leaves here 8.42 p.m., arrives at 9.35 p.m. Mind you, isn't that a bit late for you?"

"L-late? N-no. My brother's coming with me."

"Oh, I see. He's older than you then?"

"Much older," giggled Tony.

"That'll be all right then," said the man.

Tony thanked him and went over to the exit, murmuring the train times out loud. Just before he reached it, he stopped. What could the man have meant by, "That'll be all right"? Had he and the little vampire overlooked something in their plans, some problem that might arise on an evening train? I'd better ask the man, he thought, and so he retraced his steps to the counter.

"I bet you've forgotten the times," said the man in a friendly way. "Here, I've written them down for you."

"Thank you," murmured Tony in surprise, taking the scrap of paper. "I wanted to ask you something."

"Yes?"

"What did you mean when you said, 'That's all right then'?"

"I was just thinking what might happen when two young lads like you wanted to travel alone on a train at night."

"What sort of thing?" stammered Tony.

"The ticket collector would be very suspicious."

"Why?"

"Well, the pair of you might have run away from home!"

Tony was silent in dismay. He and Rudolph certainly had not thought of that.

"But there's no need to worry," said the man.

"Why?"

"Because your big brother'll be with you."

"He's not big," answered Tony gloomily. "Just older."

"Older than 18?"

"Mmmm."

"Well then. There really won't be any problem. Your brother will just have to carry his identity card."

"Identity card?"

"So he can prove his age."

"A-ah – yes."

In some confusion, Tony went back to the fir tree.

"Everything all right?" asked the little vampire.

"If you had an identity card ..."

"What's that?"

"A card which says your name is Rudolph Sackville-Bagg, that you were born on ..."

"I have got one," interrupted Rudolph.

"Really?"

"Of course."

Tony felt a weight fall from him. "Then don't forget to bring it on Saturday, for goodness' sake!"

"'Course I won't – it's in my coffin."

Tony sighed deeply, then his eyes closed and he was asleep. He did not even hear his mother come into his room and stare in disbelief at his pile of clothes.

15

Packing Up

"You seem quite excited," said Tony's mother at breakfast the following Saturday.

"Do I?" grunted Tony. It was true, he did feel a bit funny – but not because of the cases they were about to pack, nor at the thought of the farm to which he and his parents were to travel early the next day. It was the train journey with the little vampire that very evening which gave him an empty feeling in his tummy. Even the bread rolls which his father had just fetched from the baker did not take his fancy.

"You must eat properly, Tony."

"Yes." Listlessly, he spread some butter on a roll, took a small bite and chewed on it.

"Are you feeling poorly?" asked his mother.

"No!" he exclaimed.

His parents wanted to take the opportunity of going to the cinema that evening before they travelled to Nether Bogsbottom the next day. If they thought he was ill, they might stay at home instead ... and on no account must that be allowed to happen!

"I'm just a bit tired," he said, shoving half the roll hastily into his mouth. "I can eat two of these. May I?"

"Of course you can."

After breakfast he lay on his bed with a pain in

his tummy.

"Tony, have you packed yet?" called his father.

"Yes," he replied weakly.

"Don't forget your swimming things."

"No."

Tony stood up slowly. He was reminded of the wolf in the fairy story, whose stomach had been filled with stones by the seven little kids, and who ran to the well crying, "What's bumbling and rumbling around in my tum?"

He put his case on the bed and began to pack his favourite books: *Twelve Chilling Vampire Tales*, *In the House of Count Dracula*, *Vampire Stories for Advanced Readers*. On top, he put his underwear and socks, two T-shirts with long sleeves, two jerseys, pyjamas and his bathing trunks.

"I'm ready!" he called out.

"Ready?" echoed his mother from the bathroom. "That was mighty quick. I bet you've forgotten half the things you need."

"I have not!" he retorted, zipping up his case.

He heard his mother cross the hall. With what Tony called her I-know-better smile on her face, she came into his bedroom. She studied the fastened suitcase.

"You can't have put much in there," she said.

"Enough," Tony reassured her.

"Your pyjamas?"

"Of course."

"What about pants?"

59

"Yes."

"Trousers?" she asked. Without waiting for his reply, she went to the cupboard and looked inside. "Pooh, it smells so musty in here," she complained. "You must air your cupboard more, Tony."

Tony suppressed a giggle. He knew why it smelt: Rudolph's cloak was hidden under his tracksuit! But by now his mother had discovered his new jeans, still hanging on a hanger.

"Why haven't you packed these?" she asked.

"I – I must have forgotten them," he stammered.

"There you are! Always forgetting something! Just as well I checked for you!"

He could hardly tell her he had left the jeans out on purpose because he was going to take them that evening for the little vampire.

"We'll put them in now!" declared his mother, opening the case and putting the jeans in it. "Did you remember socks?" she asked, lifting Tony's clothes carefully to one side.

"Yes I did!" shouted Tony. He felt as if he were about to explode with rage. "Why do you have to go rummaging about? What am I going to give Rudolph?" In horror, he clapped his hand over his mouth. He had nearly given the game away!

His mother looked at him curiously. "I hope you weren't going to lend your new jeans to a school friend?"

"No, I-I mean, y-yes," stammered Tony. "H-he was going to swop his for mine." This wasn't true of course, but if his mother would put words into his mouth … "He's going to wear them in for me," he continued cunningly, "because I don't like jeans looking so brand new."

"Why can't you wear them in yourself?" scolded his mother, shaking her head disapprovingly. "I think it would be best if I took your case. Otherwise you'll go and put your grisly books in it. And this is meant to be a healthy holiday!"

She closed the zip decisively, locked it and put the key in her pocket.

"But Mum –" protested Tony.

"Too late," she said with a smile and went over to the door with the case. Tony wondered if she would have to open the case again. Then he realised she would only stand over him so it would be impossible to get the jeans out for Rudolph in any case.

Bother! Luckily he had not packed the book he was reading at the moment, called *Dracula*. He took it down from the shelf and stretched out on his bed. Within minutes, the events which occurred on the ship from Varna which was carrying the chests of Count Dracula to England had him so engrossed that he forgot everything else – the jeans, the locked suitcase and the unsolved problem of what trousers the little vampire was going to wear that evening.

16

Departure

At half past seven, Tony's father stood in the hall, ready to go. He wore his dark green corduroy suit, green shirt and a yellow tie.

"How much longer will you be, Hilary?" he called impatiently.

"Just five minutes," answered Tony's mother from the bathroom.

"You have got all togged up!" remarked Tony, leaning against his bedroom door. "Just to go to the cinema!"

"We're going dancing afterwards," explained his father.

Tony's heart beat with delight: they certainly would not be home before midnight in that case. But he must not let his father see how well it fitted in with his plans.

"Are you going to be out *so* late?" he said, pretending to be disappointed. "You're always going off and leaving me."

"You'll pass the time all right."

"How?"

"Watching telly, I'll bet."

"Is that okay then?"

"Yes. Until ten o'clock. You are on holiday, after all."

"Oh great," said Tony happily. If only his father knew that that evening he would be sitting, not in front of the television, but on a train!

Tony's mother came out of the bathroom.
She was wearing a white blouse and black
velvet trousers. She had also curled her hair.
Putting on her coat, she said to Tony, "Don't
read too late, will you?"

"Dad said I could watch telly."

"Oh. What's on?"

"Wh-what's on?" stuttered Tony. He had not even looked, and as he usually knew exactly what was on, she might get suspicious!

"A chat show," he said quickly, "with a quiz."

"No horror film?" she asked, still suspicious.

"No," he assured her, and had to smile. He did not need a film to make his hair stand on end this evening!

"But at half past nine, you're to go to bed. After all, you must be wide awake tomorrow when we go on holiday."

"Dad said ten o'clock."

"All right then."

It was a quarter to eight when his parents left. It was already getting dark outside. He had agreed to meet the little vampire at the cemetery at eight. If he hurried, he could be there in ten minutes. He had five minutes to spare in which to find a pair of trousers for the little vampire, to pack the cloak which lay in his cupboard in a bag, and to fetch the tickets ...

17

Rudolph's New Clothes

Shortly after eight o'clock, Tony darted down the dark pathway which led to the cemetery. Thick bushes grew on either side; they rippled and rustled and seemed to be stretching out their branches to touch him. Tony gave a sudden shout: something soft had streaked between his legs and vanished into the bushes with a cry. He began to run.

At the edge of the path, half hidden in the bushes, stood a bench. In some alarm, Tony saw that it was occupied. Someone was sitting there in the darkness … Tony's heart was in his mouth … suppose it was Aunt Dorothy? But as he drew nearer, he realised there were two figures on the bench … a pair of lovebirds in each other's arms, and they certainly were not taking any notice of him!

He hurried past. Only when he saw the old cemetery wall in front of him did he breathe a sigh of relief. The vampire should be waiting for him in the undergrowth.

"Rudolph?" he called.

There was a rustling in the bushes, twigs snapped. Then a small figure swathed in a cloak stepped out into the path.

"You?" said Tony in surprise.

"Hi, Tony!" said Anna with a smile.

"I …" he murmured, searching for something to say. On no account must he ask after

Rudolph straight away if he did not want to annoy her. He knew how touchy she was. "... How nice to see you," he said, hoping he sounded convincing.

"Really?" She beamed at him. "Nicer than seeing Rudolph?"

"Well," he said evasively, "I was due to meet him, actually."

"I know," she laughed. "He's waiting for you. He sent me on ahead because he did not want to leave his coffin unguarded. Come on."

She took his arm and led him between the bushes over to the cemetery wall. There, in its shadow, Rudolph sat waiting on his coffin.

"You're late," he said gruffly.

"I didn't know which trousers to bring for you," explained Tony. "I was going to bring my jeans, but Mum packed them."

"So what am I going to wear?" growled the little vampire.

Shamefacedly, Tony pulled from the hessian bag the only pair of trousers he could think of to bring: the leather knee breeches from Austria. His grandmother had taken his brown cords away with her, because she was going to sew patches on the knees, and the black linen trousers were at the cleaners. "These," he said, holding them by their gaily embroidered pinafore. Anna, standing near him giggled softly. She obviously thought the trousers just as ridiculous as he did.

"I hadn't got any others," he said apologetically.

But the little vampire seemed to like the trousers. He stroked the rough leather and the embroidery with his skinny fingers.

"Pretty," he said.

Anna laughed out loud.

"You're just jealous!" hissed the little vampire. "But they're *my* trousers! Tony brought them for me!" Quickly, he put them on.

Tony had to hold his hand in front of his mouth to stop himself laughing. The breeches, with their embroidered pinafore, were too big for Rudolph even with his cloak tucked into them, and their braces hung loosely on his lean shoulders. With his chalk-white face, hair dangling to his shoulders, and his spindly legs in holey stockings sticking out below the breeches, he looked just like a scarecrow!

Perhaps he'd look a little less of a fright if he wore the little jerkin that went with it, thought Tony. He had packed it just in case, together with the Tyrolean hat which went so well with the outfit, or so his grandmother said. He groped in the bag and pulled out the jerkin.

"This goes with it," he said, "if you want it..."

"Oh yes!" cried the little vampire. He put it on quickly and his face lit up. "Great!" he enthused, pulling at the silver buttons which glinted in the moonlight.

Tony bit back a laugh. Anna giggled furtively. "You look as if you're off to a fancy dress party!"

"Oh really? You're just jealous!"

"There's something else," said Tony and took out the felt hat with its green feather.

The vampire was over the moon. Smiling happily, he pulled the hat over his shaggy hair. "I've always wanted a hat with a feather like this!" he said, and paraded proudly round the coffin, while Anna and Tony looked on, making faces in their efforts not to laugh out loud. Compared with what he looked like as a "normal" vampire, Rudolph now looked rather comic, thought Tony. And that was probably just as well, if they were going on a train.

Going on a train ... He realised with a start that their train left at 8.42! And they would need at least ten minutes to get to the station with the heavy coffin!

"Our train's due soon. Come on, Rudolph, hurry up!"

"Take it easy," replied Rudolph. "In any case, my hat isn't on quite right."

"We'll be late!"

"Nonsense!" growled the vampire, adjusting his hat.

"Typical!" hissed Anna. "I'll have to carry the coffin myself!"

With that, she picked up the coffin by its middle. Her tiny thin legs almost buckling under the weight, she squared her narrow shoulders and set off. Tony ran after her.

"Can I help?"

"No," she smiled. "I can manage."

"Wait!" called the little vampire. "I can't go so fast with my hat on!"

18

Wrapping Paper

On the way, the little vampire suddenly called out: "Wait a minute! We've got to wrap up the coffin in some paper!"

Startled, Anna came to a standstill and put the coffin down.

"Have you got the paper?"

"Tony's got it."

Tony went cold. "Me?"

"That's what we arranged," growled the vampire. "You were going to bring something for me to wear – plus some wrapping paper."

Tony shook his head vigorously. "I certainly was not. We had only talked about the clothes."

"Didn't I mention we would need some paper to wrap the coffin in?"

"Yes, you did. But you didn't say I was to get it."

"Bah!" said the vampire furiously. "What are we going to do now?"

"Perhaps you can buy some paper at the station," suggested Anna.

"No," said Tony, "they don't sell it."

"If the coffin isn't wrapped, I'm staying here!" threatened the vampire.

"With George the Boisterous?" retorted Tony with a grin. This time he was not going to let himself be bullied, because he knew just how much the little vampire was counting on coming!

"No, no," the little vampire gave in. "I'm
coming with you, of course – but my coffin!"
he wailed. "If someone finds it, I'm lost!"

In the meantime, Anna had walked around
the coffin and had studied it from all sides. "I
don't think it looks like a coffin," she said,
"more like a chest."

"Sailors have chests like that," said Tony.

"But I'm not a sailor," protested the little vampire.

"You certainly don't look like one," giggled Anna, looking at the Austrian national costume and Tyrolean hat.

"Even so, you could own a chest like that," said Tony. "And now, we really should get going, if we're not going to miss the train."

Together, he and Anna carried the coffin as far as the brightly lit entrance to the station.

"I hope it's all going to be all right," worried the little vampire, following along on shaky legs. He was so scared he had not even noticed that his hat was quite lop-sided.

"Couldn't you just ask?" he beseeched Tony, when they had put the coffin down behind a bush.

"Ask what?"

"Whether they do sell wrapping paper. Th-there are always kiosks at railway stations."

Tony looked up at the station clock. It was twenty-eight minutes past eight. "Okay. But don't expect too much."

Annoyed at having let himself be persuaded, Tony went over to the station entrance hall. Why should any of the kiosks even be open? They had all been closed the Sunday before.

In the entrance hall, his gaze fell first on two ladies, standing at the ticket office. They were wearing green woollen overcoats, Tyrolean hats and walking shoes. He had to laugh: they went so beautifully with Rudolph's outfit! If they all sat in the same compartment, they could be mistaken for three characters advertising the joys of Austria!

Then he noticed that the little stall opposite was lit up. A man sat behind the glass.

"Do you have any wrapping paper?" asked Tony.

"I did have some," said the man, "but whether it's still here or not ..." He opened a drawer, peered inside and shook his head.

"Sorry. Must have been sold."

"What about that, up on the shelf?" asked Tony, who had spied a brightly coloured roll.

"That's shelf-lining paper," said the man.

"Can I have it?"

"I wanted to line my shelves with it."

"*Please!*"

The man hesitated. He took down the roll and looked at it. "I always did think the pattern was a bit too brash," he said.

"Fantastic!" Tony was delighted. "How much is it?"

It was just as well he had brought some money with him.

"Nothing," said the man. "I'll give it to you – with this little piece of ribbon as well." He brought a card with green ribbon wrapped round it out of a drawer.

"Thanks a lot," said Tony in surprise. "If ever I need more wrapping paper, I'll make sure I come to you!"

"Better not!" laughed the man. "The next shelf-lining paper I buy is sure to go on my shelves!"

19

Wrapping Up a Coffin

"You did get some!" beamed the little vampire, as Tony returned with the roll of paper and the ribbon.

"Mmmm," muttered Tony. He had no wish to get into a discussion as to the difference between wrapping paper and shelf-lining paper. Instead he gave the little vampire the roll. "There you are!"

"What? Me?" cried the vampire.

"You wanted to wrap up the coffin!"

"But –" The vampire looked imploringly at Anna. "I'm no good at it. I'm bound to rip the paper or something!"

"Well, you'll just have to be careful!" said Tony with a grin, enjoying the sudden feeling of superiority.

"We'll help you," said Anna. She lifted up one end of the coffin. "You must wrap the paper round and round the coffin like a bandage," she explained.

"Okay, okay," grunted the vampire. With a pained expression, he began to unroll the paper. His hat slipped over his eyes. He looked so funny that Anna and Tony had to laugh. The vampire flung the hat furiously to the grass. "It's all very well for you to laugh!" he shouted. "But you don't even think of giving me a hand!"

"What do you mean?" contradicted Anna

73

hotly. "I'm holding up the coffin for you!"

"But Tony's just standing there grinning!"

"If it weren't for me, you wouldn't have any wrapping paper!" retorted Tony as an excuse. How many times had the vampire just looked on without lifting a finger when he and Anna had struggled over something? For instance, when he had installed himself in Tony's basement storeroom, hiding his coffin behind some planks of wood – and then Tony's father had decided he needed those very planks! The vampire had nearly driven Tony to despair with his "tiredness" and his lack of concern. Now Tony had the upper hand for once – but in spite of this, he did not take advantage of it.

"I'll give you a hand," he offered placatingly. "You go over there."

Obediently, the little vampire went to the other side of the coffin and waited till Tony had unrolled enough paper to reach him. With Anna holding the coffin up, the little vampire took the roll and unravelled enough paper to reach back under the coffin to Tony. Tony unrolled a bit more, and handed it back over the coffin to Rudolph. Soon they had the whole thing wrapped up. Anna pulled the ribbon round the middle and tied a bow.

"Doesn't it look great!"

"Just like a birthday present," agreed Tony.

The little vampire sighed deeply. "No one would guess there's a coffin in there." With a contented smile, he stooped and picked up his hat. "Shall we go?"

"Not me," said Anna.

Tony turned to her in surprise. "Aren't you coming onto the platform?"

Silently she shook her head. Her eyes had grown large and brimmed with tears. "Good luck, Tony!" she said softly. "See you."

With that, she spread her cloak and before Tony had got over his surprise, she had flown away.

"She didn't even wish me luck!" grumbled the little vampire. "And I might never come back!"

Tony had to laugh. Rudolph Sackville-Bagg was – jealous!

"She leaves everything to me!" grizzled the little vampire. "She might at least have carried the coffin as far as the train!"

"It was most certainly in order to help you that she didn't offer!" retorted Tony.

"What do you mean?"

"So she would not draw attention to us. She wasn't wearing human clothes, don't forget!"

"Oh I see," agreed the little vampire. "I'd almost forgotten." He looked down at himself proudly. "I'm not a vampire any more. No, I'm –" He paused and then said complacently, "Rudolph Sackville-Bagg the Beautiful!"

Tony just managed to smother a smile. "We must hurry!" he said. "The train leaves in two minutes."

The vampire jumped. "Good grief!" he said, running round to the end of the coffin. "Come on, Tony!"

Tony stood still. "What about saying please?" he lectured.

"Okay, please," growled the little vampire through clenched teeth. "Will you come now?"

"With pleasure," said Tony graciously, and lifted the other end of the coffin.

20

I Love to Go A-Wandering!

As they crossed the station entrance hall, the man in the kiosk was busy rearranging the bottles on his shelves, and had his back to them. The woman at the ticket office sat bowed over a book, writing something, and gave them only a quick glance betraying not a trace of surprise or alarm. The vampire obviously did not look out of the ordinary to her. Other than them, there was no one about. Tony breathed a sigh of relief: he had imagined running the gauntlet of distrustful eyes on every side as they crossed the entrance hall.

Even on the platform, it was obvious he need not have worried. Apart from the two ladies in green woollen overcoats, who wandered slowly up and down and did not spare them a glance, they were the only people waiting for the train.

"They've got fantastic hats on!" said the little vampire, pointing to the two ladies.

"Don't stare at them so!" said Tony. "Otherwise they'll get suspicious."

"Their hats are much smarter than mine," sulked the little vampire. "They've got hair, not a feather."

"*What?*"

"Hair. It looks like a shaving brush."

Now it was Tony's turn to peer curiously in

77

the ladies' direction. Their hats were indeed adorned with a short thick tuft of hair. "That's from a chamois' beard. That's a sort of mountain goat."

The vampire pulled a face. "Yuk! Goats!" he

shrieked. "We vampires hate goats!" He stroked the feather in his hat tenderly. "But we do like birds. After all, we are related to them."

His outcry seemed to have startled the two ladies. They had come to a standstill and were looking over at them curiously. Quickly Tony placed himself in front of the little vampire and began to whistle a tune: "I love to go a-wandering along the mountain track ..." From the corner of his eye, he saw the ladies exchange looks. Then they shook their heads in bewilderment and resumed their stroll.

At that moment, the train arrived. It boomed and thundered, its brakes screeched. The vampire stared at the long carriages in fascination. "A train, a real train," he murmured, entranced.

"If you spend so long looking at it, it'll leave without you," remarked Tony bitingly. He had seen the two ladies get into the first carriage. The vampire's pale face turned even whiter.

"Oh no – anything but that!" he said, grabbed his coffin by the middle and carried it to the train. Tony only had to run after him and hold the carriage door open.

21

Choosing a Compartment

"Made it!" sighed the vampire when they had climbed into the third to last carriage and put the coffin down near the door.

"Not yet," countered Tony.

"What do you mean?"

"Well, we can't stay here in the corridor!"

The vampire looked puzzled. "Why not?"

"Because too many people will come past. We must go and sit in a compartment. I'll go and see if I can find one that's empty."

"What about me?" said the little vampire plaintively.

"You wait here."

"What if someone comes?"

"You can disappear into the toilet." Tony pointed to the door marked W.C. "You can lock yourself in and I'll knock three times when I come back."

"What about my coffin?"

"Coffin? What coffin?" grinned Tony. "Or are you talking about this large, beautifully wrapped surprise present?"

But the vampire was in no mood for jokes. With dignity, he declared: "I shall not leave my coffin unguarded. Certainly not in a –" He was going to say "train", but at that moment the train started with a jerk. The vampire took a couple of unsteady steps and then found himself sitting on his coffin. Surprised and speechless, he looked at Tony, who was having difficulty in keeping a straight face. But how was the vampire to know you should hold on tight when a train starts to move? He had never been on one before.

"You'd better stay sitting here till I come back," said Tony. "I won't be long."

"Mmmm," nodded the vampire. He seemed only too glad not to have to stand up. It was obvious that the swaying and rattling of the carriage upset him. "But hurry up!" he pleaded.

Tony pushed open the door between the carriages. He wanted to be like a hero in a television film, all easy-going and nonchalant. He pulled the corners of his mouth down and tried to look cool and unshakeable as he sauntered down the corridor with the long, swaying strides of a cowboy. After all, it was nearly nine o'clock, and on no account must he look like a frightened little schoolboy.

However, sadly there was no audience for his dramatic display. In the first compartment a woman sat by the window, her head tilted back, obviously asleep. In the second compartment, there was a man reading a newspaper, and Tony could only see his legs. The other compartments were empty.

Tony decided on the fourth one. If by chance someone else boarded the train on the way, they would surely go into one of the first empty compartments, he thought.

"Did you find one?" asked the vampire in

excitement when Tony came back.

Tony gave a superior smile. "Come and see," he said.

22

Safe!

With a nervous look at the swaying floor, the vampire stood up. "Is it far?"

Tony had to smile. "Just four compartments," he said.

The vampire lifted one end of the coffin with a sigh. Tony took the other end. It seemed to him that the coffin had grown heavier and more unwieldy, as together they carried it down the corridor to their compartment. There, Tony quickly shut the door. Now they were safe – for a while! The vampire seemed to think so too. With a sigh of relief, he sank onto a seat and stretched out.

"What about your coffin?" asked Tony.

"What about it?"

"We can't leave it between the seats."

"Where shall we put it?"

"In the luggage rack."

The vampire looked around the compartment in bewilderment. "Luggage rack? What's that?"

"That shelf thing up there," explained Tony impatiently. "It's called a luggage rack."

"Oh I see," said the little vampire. "Well, if you think so ..." He took off his hat, stroked the feather lovingly and laid it on the seat beside him. Then he crossed his legs comfortably. "You can put it up there," he said. "I've no objection!"

Tony's mouth dropped open in astonishment. "M-me?" he cried. "Do you really think I can hoist this mammoth great thing up there on my own?"

The vampire threw him a pitying look before condescending to get up. "Yes, just what I thought," he said, taking the coffin and lifting it up onto the rack apparently without effort. "You see, it's quite easy."

"But you always make out you're so weak!" said Tony indignantly.

"It all depends on whether I've had something to eat or not," said the vampire from up on the seat.

Tony shuddered. "S-so you've already eaten today?"

"Of course," said the little vampire, running his tongue over his lips at the memory. "Or would you prefer me to find something here on the train ...?"

"No, no!" cried Tony in horror.

He realised that he felt quite peculiar. He suddenly had the feeling that there was a certain menace in the vampire's little red eyes which seemed to bore into his neck ... But surely the vampire was his friend? Tony gulped. "I – er, I brought something with me," he stammered, pulling a flat box from the inside pocket of his jacket. "Catch the Hat!"

"Catch the what?" asked the vampire hoarsely.

"Catch the Hat!" repeated Tony anxiously.

To his relief, the vampire said, "But I like hats!" stroking his pride and joy.

At home, when Tony had put in the game, he had felt a bit stupid: imagine playing "Catch the Hat!" on a train with a vampire! But now he was glad they would have something to pass the time with – just to keep the vampire's mind occupied!

Rudolph studied the box. "Does one of us win?" he growled.

"Of course." Tony was quick to reassure him.

"Okay then. Let's start."

23

Vampire Hats

Tony sat down opposite the vampire by the window. He took the board out of the box, put it on the table between them and indicated the little hats. "Which colour do you want to be?"

The vampire burst into grating laughter. "Red, what do you think?"

A shudder ran down Tony's spine. He said nothing, however, just pushed the red "home" circle and the four little red hats round towards the vampire. For himself, he put the yellow hats on the yellow circle.

"How do we play?" growled the vampire.

"I'll show you," said Tony, taking a red and a yellow hat and putting them on the board with three squares between them.

"You catch me if you throw a four," he explained, "like this." He put the dice down with the four showing, took the red hat, moved it forward four spaces and clapped it over the yellow hat. "Now the yellow one's caught!"

The vampire smiled with pleasure. "What do I do with my prisoners?" he asked.

"You have to try to get them back to your 'home'," answered Tony, pointing to the red circle.

"And then what happens to them?" The vampire's eyes glistened in expectation.

"Nothing," replied Tony, taken aback by

the question. "At the end, we count up who has the most hats, and that person's the winner."

"Only count them up?" The vampire sounded disappointed. "These human games of yours aren't very exciting."

"What do you mean?" said Tony, puzzled.

"We'll have to make up new rules!" The little vampire pointed to the little golden hat which was still in the box. "What's that for?" he asked.

"Dunno," replied Tony.

The vampire picked up the hat and twisted it between his skinny fingers.

"I've got an idea," he said.

"What?"

"This little golden hat can be a vampire hat."

"A vampire hat?" Tony did not understand.

"Any hat that's bitten – er, I mean caught – becomes a vampire hat," explained the vampire and giggled. "In the end, all there'll be are vampire hats – that sounds fun, doesn't it?"

"Well," said Tony evasively. He was not actually convinced by the vampire's idea. "We could try it."

Eagerly, the vampire pushed his four red hats over to Tony, so that he now had eight. In the middle of the red circle, the vampire put the golden hat.

"You can throw first," he said happily.

Tony threw a six. He took one of the yellow hats and moved it forward six spaces.

Then Rudolph threw a two. "Hey, that's not fair!" he raged, and tried to throw again.

"I'm next!" protested Tony, and reached for the dice. With bad grace, the little vampire moved his golden hat two spaces.

Then Tony threw a five.

The vampire counted with a finger how many spaces now lay between the two hats. "Three," he murmured. "I've almost got you."

He threw. It was a six! "Drat!" he said and moved on six spaces.

Tony bit his lip so as not to laugh and threw: a three!

The vampire jumped.

"I've won!" shouted Tony with ill-disguised triumph. The vampire's mouth began to twitch.

"Won?" he repeated with menace in his voice. "There was a trick in it somewhere!"

"There was not!" retorted Tony. "I was just luckier with my throws!"

"Luck! Luck!" spat the vampire, staring at Tony with wickedly gleaming eyes. "Shall I show you what I think of your rotten game?"

With that, he hit the board so hard that it spun through the air and came to land on the floor between the seats. The hats were scattered all over the seats and floor, and the dice landed over by the compartment door. Tony's first reaction was to jump to his feet in anger. Then he told himself that that was exactly what the vampire wanted him to do, so he stayed sitting quietly and looked out of the window. Outside, it had grown quite dark, and he counted the lights as they went past.

As he had predicted, his apparent calm
confused the vampire. He fidgeted uneasily
on his seat and looked at Tony. After a while
he asked: "Aren't you cross?"

"No," lied Tony. With secret glee he added,

"I'm just wondering whether I might go and sit in another compartment."

"What?" cried the vampire. "In another compartment? What would happen to me?"

Tony had to grin. "We only fight when we're together. I'm sure you'd rather be on your own."

"No!" shouted the vampire. His lips trembled and his little red eyes flickered. "I-I don't know h-how to behave on a train," he stammered.

"I suppose not," agreed Tony.

"And anyway, I – I'm helpless without you."

Tony smiled, flattered. "Well, if that's the case," he said craftily, "perhaps you had better be a bit more polite to me."

"I will, I will," said the vampire hastily.

"Good," said Tony. "Then you can begin by picking up the game."

24

Rudolph Tells a Tale

After he had collected the game together, the vampire asked, unusually politely for him, "Shall we have another game?"

"Oh," said Tony, "it wasn't that good."

"But what if we play your way?"

"No. There's no point."

"Why not?"

"You always have to win."

"Me?" protested the vampire with feeling. "You started it. You were the one who said we must count who had the most hats!"

"And who asked whether there could be a winner of the game?" retorted Tony.

"You did, of course!" said the vampire.

Tony temporarily lost his tongue at such impudence. Then he said crossly, "You're just like your brother Greg – he can't bear to lose either!"

But instead of looking put out, the vampire looked very pleased, and smiled. "Do you think so? I wish Greg had heard you say that." He added thoughtfully, "He always maintains I'm degenerate. The white sheep of the family, so to speak."

"You?" said Tony scornfully. "Never!"

"Yes, yes, that's what he says." The little vampire leaned back in his seat and crossed his legs. "Once Greg and I were instructed by the Family Council to teach McRookery a lesson," he began. "We were to go to his house at midnight and ring the bell. Brrr!" He shivered at the memory.

Tony could well imagine how the vampire must have felt, because he too could not think of the nightwatchman without horror. His one ambition was to get rid of the vampires and their tomb, and therefore he always carried with him especially sharpened stakes of wood and a hammer when he did his rounds of the cemetery.

"What happened?" asked Tony.

"I was supposed to entice him out of the house. I was to call: 'Mr McRookery! Your woodshed's on fire!' Then Greg was supposed to bite him. Just a little one, just to teach him a lesson. And I was to write on the door in red:

"McRookery might as well be blind:
Our vampire tomb he'll never find!"

"Well –" The vampire was obviously delighted with Tony's attention. "I rang the bell ... nothing happened. Nearby, Greg stirred in the bushes and my knees felt quite weak. I pushed the doorbell again. The harsh sound rang shrilly through the silence that engulfed us ..."

"Hey, don't keep me in suspense!" cried Tony.

"Then suddenly: footsteps! Slow shuffling footsteps! They came nearer and nearer. Then someone coughed. I felt quite sick ..."

"Me too," murmured Tony.

"Then I heard McRookery's grating voice. 'Who is it?' he asked. Such a wave of garlic

fumes came through the cracks round the
door and swamped me that I nearly passed
out. I wanted to speak, but I couldn't. I
couldn't make a sound. Then Greg called: 'Mr
McRookery! Your woodshed's on fire!' At
that very moment, the door opened. But it
wasn't McRookery who faced me –"

"It wasn't?"

"It was something with eyes like glowing
coals. It gave a cry which chilled me to the
marrow, sprang – and landed on my shoulder!"

Tony stared open-mouthed at the vampire.
"On your shoulder? How big was it?"

The vampire lowered his head. "It was a
cat," he said shamefacedly.

"A cat?" Tony could not believe it.

"Yes. McRookery's cat. He was clever enough to stay in the shadow of the door so I would only see his cat's glowing eyes as he held it in his arms. When he recognised who it was at the door, he threw the cat at me!" The vampire stopped. There were beads of sweat on his pale forehead. "I was so scared I ran away without turning round once. 'Just wait till I catch you, you rascal!' I heard McRookery call after me, but I ran faster than I'd ever run before."

"How do you know it was a cat?" asked Tony.

"Greg told me later. He was able to see it all from behind the bush without McRookery seeing him. And ever since, I've been the white sheep of the family because I took to my heels because of a cat!" His face wore such a doleful expression that Tony had to laugh.

"I'd have been scared too," he said, trying to console the vampire. "Anyway, I think it was brave of you even to ring on McRookery's door."

"Really?" The vampire began to smile again.

"Yes, I do. And everyone's scared at some time."

"Even a vampire," said the little vampire with a sigh.

25

A Nasty Surprise

The vampire picked up his hat and put it on again. "You're a real friend," he said warmly. "I can tell from the fantastic clothes you've given me." His gaze slid lovingly over the jerkin and leather breeches. "You have given them to me, haven't you?"

"Given?" Tony had to laugh. "I'd dearly love to. But I don't think my mother or granny would be very pleased.." He stopped and looked towards the door of the compartment. "Did you hear anything?"

"No," said the little vampire. "Only this terrible clatter."

"Someone's coming," whispered Tony.

The vampire froze. "In here?"

"Perhaps it's the ticket collector." Suddenly Tony remembered what he had been meaning to ask the little vampire. "Did you bring your identity card?"

"Of course," said the vampire proudly. "It's in my coffin."

"In your coffin?" cried Tony.

The vampire looked startled. "That's the safest place for it.'

"Oh no!" groaned Tony, and held his head. Why hadn't he asked about it sooner? "And what exactly are you going to do when the ticket collector comes and asks to see your identity card?"

"Ah –" At last the vampire seemed to under-stand. "You mean we've wrapped the coffin up ..."

"Exactly! You'll have to unwrap it and then the ticket collector will see it isn't a parcel at all."

The vampire's eyes opened wide in anxiety. "D-do you really think so?" he pleaded. "What can we do?"

"No idea," replied Tony, but then the compartment door opened and a lady, blink-ing in a friendly fashion, looked in.

"Is there a space in here with you?" she asked.

26

Poyson – With a "Y"

Tony and the little vampire looked at each other in alarm.

"Well, er –" began Tony. Somehow, he must stop her from sitting in their compartment – but how? If he was too rude, there was always the risk she would complain about him to the ticket collector. "Er, you know –"

However, the lady seemed to take Tony's hesitation to mean the opposite. "That's very kind of you," she said, and came right in.

Tony's heart nearly stopped beating. "B-but..." he stuttered, looking imploringly at the little vampire for help. But Rudolph simply watched darkly as the lady brought in a suitcase, a basket and a plastic carrier bag and put them up in the luggage rack. Then she shut the door and sat down in the seat next to it, two away from Tony.

She did not seem to notice how unwelcome she was, because she said happily: "Thank goodness for that, a no-smoking compartment! I'm sure I'll feel at home in here with you. Do you know, I've just been in a compartment with two gentlemen, two very nice gentlemen, but after only a very short while they began to smoke! And as I cannot abide smoke, I had to leave!" She beamed and sniffed the air exploratively.

"It smells very odd in here too," she remarked. "I expect it's the old upholstery. Anyway, my name's Mrs Poyson – with a 'y'. What are yours?"

"Ours?"

"Yes." She turned to Tony and looked at him with her extraordinary blinking eyes. "I can't see you properly,"she said suddenly. "Everything is so blurred. She reached to her face and cried out. "Oh, my glasses! I haven't got my glasses on!" She began to grope frantically in her handbag.

Tony bit his lip, because he could see exactly where her glasses were! One corner of them was sticking out of the breast pocket of her jacket!

The vampire had also noticed and indicated as much to Tony with a meaningful nod of his head.

"Where can they be?" she murmured to herself. "Perhaps I left them at my daughter's. Yes, that must be it. I must have left them lying around there."

Tony giggled furtively. He felt rather mean not telling her where her glasses were, but on the other hand, it would be much safer for the little vampire and himself to share a compartment with someone who could not see properly.

Tony now dared look at her more closely. How old could she be? She was certainly younger than Granny, and she was over sixty. In any case, she did not look like Granny, he thought. She was wearing a trouser suit, a colourful scarf, a string of pearls and huge earrings. And her very blond hair must be dyed, he decided.

27

Not Something to Joke About

At last the lady snapped her bag shut and sighed. "Luckily I've got a spare pair at home," she said.

Tony and the little vampire looked at each other and exchanged conspiratorial smiles. But their cheerfulness was short-lived.

"What did you say your name was?" asked the lady.

"My – name?" replied Tony, looking imploringly at the little vampire, but he just shrugged his shoulders helplessly.

"Er, well, I'm Tony Peasbody, and this –" he said hesitatingly, "this is my brother, Rudolph Sackville-Bagg."

"Brothers! How nice! Why have you got different surnames?"

"Different sur –? Oh yes." He had not thought of that. Then an excuse occurred to him. "Our mother married twice. My brother comes from her first marriage. He's *much* older than me."

Tony had emphasised the "much" so heavily that the lady asked with amusement: "*So* much older? How old is he then?"

That gave Tony a shock. What should he say?

"Fourteen," replied the vampire in a hollow voice.

"Only fourteen?" she exclaimed with a

laugh. "So you're just children! What were your Christian names? Tony and –"

"Rudolph," growled the vampire.

"Tony and Rudolph! And I thought you were grown-ups! My silly old eyes! Should you be out alone at night then? Won't your mother be worried about you?"

"No she won't!" crowed the vampire.

Tony added quickly, "You see, we're going to our aunt in the country."

"Oh. And where is that?"

"Nether Bogsbottom."

"Nether Bogsbottom?" she replied in surprise. "Then we're going to the same destination."

"Oh," said Tony. "Are you going to Nether Bogsbottom too?"

She laughed. "No. I get out at Upper Bogsbottom just like you. I live at Mildwater, a nearby village."

"That's all we need!" hissed Tony to the little vampire.

"What's your aunt's name?"

"M-my aunt?" Tony jumped. Of course he had quite forgotten the name of the family they were going to spend their holiday with. All he knew was that they lived at number 13, Old Street – but naturallly he was not going to tell the lady that!

"I don't remember her surname," he said. "We just call her Auntie Jane." He guessed there were probably several women with the Christian name Jane in Nether Bogsbottom, so the lady would not realise he was telling her a fib.

"Jane. Jane." She was thinking. "Not Jane Twitter?"

Tony bit his lip so as not to laugh, and shook his head.

"Jane Greatflower?"

"No."

"Oh well," she said. "I don't know that many people in Nether Bogsbottom. Mildwater is about twenty kilometres away."

What luck! Tony grinned at the little vampire.

"Your aunt will be picking you up from the station I expect."

"Er – why?"

"Well, it's over a kilometre to Nether Bogsbottom.

"Mmmm. Yes." Tony looked for help at the little vampire, but he simply sat cracking his fingers nervously.

"Otherwise we could easily take you there. My husband will be meeting me with the car."

"No, no, thank you very much," Tony said hastily. "Of course my aunt will be meeting us. Also, I'm sure our package wouldn't fit into your car." He pointed to the coffin in its wrapping paper.

The lady blinked. "My word! That is quite a parcel!"

"There's a lot in it," explained Tony. "Everything it's difficult to buy in the country: shirts, trousers, handkerchiefs, toothbrushes, socks, after shave lotion –" He stopped, unable to think of anything else.

The vampire took over with a grin: "– And blood! Blood in bottles, blood in jars, blood in tins ...!"

"I beg your pardon?" said the lady in astonishment.

"My brother is only joking," Tony said quickly to reassure her.

"You shouldn't joke about things like that," said the lady severely. "Blood is a very precious thing. It's our life's source. But I'm sure you children don't understand these things. Or do you know what our bodies need blood for?"

"Do I know what our bodies –" Tony paused. He glared at the vampire. "No."

"Well, I'll tell you. Blood provides our bodies with nourishment and oxygen. I know, because I used to be a blood donor."

"A blood donor?" At once, the little vampire's eyes glazed over and his teeth clicked together. "Was your blood very good then?"

She laughed complacently. "Yes, it was. And there was always plenty of it."

"But you're not a donor any more?" asked the vampire in a rough, throaty voice.

"No."

"Then you must be full up with blood?"

"Yes." She smiled.

Luckily she did not seem to have noticed that Rudolph had bared his terrible pointed teeth and now, with an enraptured expression on his face, was inching himself out of his seat.

For a moment, Tony was paralysed with shock. Then he jumped up, threw himself on the vampire and pushed him back onto his seat.

"Rudolph!" he cried, shaking him.

"What is it?" asked the lady anxiously. "Is your brother feeling ill after all this talk of blood? He's a little squeamish, I expect."

"Yes, yes," agreed Tony quickly. "Very squeamish. Especially when he hasn't eaten very much."

"Oh, he's hungry, is he?" she said. "If that's all the matter is!" She stood up and took down her basket from the luggage rack. "I've got plenty to eat in here!"

28

Three to Supper

The lady laid a white cloth on the seat between Tony and herself, and began to spread out the contents of her basket: two ham rolls, two cheese rolls, three hard-boiled eggs, two apples, two tomatoes, a bar of mint chocolate and a thermos flask. Everything looked so good that Tony's mouth began to water. At home, he had hardly been able to eat tea because he was so nervous, and had only had a cup of tea and a biscuit. Now his stomach rumbled.

"Just tuck in!" invited the lady.

"Thank you," said Tony and took a cheese roll.

"What about your brother? What would he like?"

"Him? He'll have a ham roll."

The vampire lifted his hands in protest, but Tony gave him the roll firmly. "Just take it," he hissed. "You don't really have to eat it."

The vampire looked with disgust at the roll in his hand, with a thick slice of ham peeping out of the edge of it. "What am I supposed to do with this?" he whispered.

Tony threw a worried look at the lady before answering, but luckily she was busy pouring coffee from the thermos into a mug and was not paying any attention to them.

"You can give it to me," he whispered back.

"Okay." The vampire gave a sigh of relief.

The lady took a sip of coffee and asked, "Tastes good?"

"Mmmm," answered the vampire. With that, he slipped the roll back to Tony who munched it happily.

"I am pleased. I suppose your mother hadn't given you anything to take with you?"

"Mm – no," mumbled Tony with his mouth full.

She shook her head disapprovingly. "You children have to be taken care of. Well – now you've got me!" she added with a smile. "You can call me Auntie Gertie! But you're not eating anything!"

"Yes, yes, we are," said Tony, taking an apple. He had nearly choked at the words "Auntie Gertie"!

"What about Rudolph? Is he full up already?" She blinked uncertainly in Rudolph's direction.

"Not quite," said the vampire in a croaky voice.

"He'd just like a tomato," said Tony hastily.

"Only a tomato?" She took a paper plate out of the basket. "Even though he was almost fainting with hunger? No, no! I'll get something really nice together for him!"

She put an egg, an apple, a tomato, two squares of chocolate and the second ham roll on the plate and passed it to Tony. "Here! This will do your brother good!"

Tony had to bite his tongue in order not to laugh. The plate quivered in his hand as he handed it to the little vampire.

"Thank you, Auntie Gertie," groaned the little vampire. He put the plate down on the little table near the "Catch the Hat" game, and pretended to eat, while handing the chocolate surreptitiously back to Tony.

"Do you often travel alone on the train?" asked the lady.

"Us? Oh no," replied Tony.

"We usually fly," said the vampire with a grating laugh.

"Your brother's quite a joker!" The lady was beginning to sound annoyed.

"Idiot!" mouthed Tony at the vampire. Turning to the lady, he said: "You mustn't take him so seriously. He's going through a difficult stage, or so my mum says."

She nodded understandingly. "Oh, yes. Of course."

Luckily she could not see the furious faces Rudolph was making as he felt his vanity had been wounded.

"But it will soon pass," she continued. "In a year at the most, your brother will be such a nice young man!"

29

Just Stories

"… Just like the young man in the book I'm reading, the lawyer – now, what was his name?"

She took a book from her bag and leafed through it, only to shut it again crossly. "Oh I can't possibly find it without my glasses!"

The book had aroused Tony's curiosity: it had a black cover with a bat on it! He twisted his head to try to read the title.

"The book's meant to be very exciting," continued the lady. "My daughter gave it to me – she read the whole thing in one night! It's about a young Englishman who is sent on business to the Carpathian Mountains. He has to visit a strange count in his castle –"

"Like Count Dracula?" cried Tony breathlessly. Even the vampire was listening.

The lady was surprised. "Do you know the book?" she asked.

"Sort of," said Tony shamefacedly. There was no need for her to know it was his favourite story.

"Do you like reading these exciting stories too?" The lady's voice took on an enthusiastic ring. "My daughter and I are mad about horror stories. But they must be really grisly ones, enough to send a shiver down your spine. What's more, it's best to read them after dark, with the wind howling round the house and everything rustling and whispering mysteriously…" She gave a deep sigh. "We're especially fond of vampire stories. They're so –" She paused for the right word. "So romantic!"

The little vampire gave a hollow laugh. It was actually far from romantic to be a vampire! "They're just stories," he said with a growl.

"And thank the Lord for that!" she laughed. "That's the best thing about them! You can read the most terrifying things but you know all the time that they're just made up."

"Just made up?" said the vampire huskily.

"There aren't really such things as spooks and ghosts, or even vampires –"

"Oh? Don't you think so?" cried the vampire.

The lady laughed. "Do you really believe there are corpses who rise from their graves by night to suck the blood of the living? I don't!"

The vampire gave a soft, dangerous rattle, while Tony gestured frantically to him to keep calm and quiet, and not let himself be irritated.

The lady did not seem to notice a thing. She want on happily: "Or perhaps you've met a vampire? A moth-eaten old thing with a deathly pale face and pointed teeth?"

She broke off, for the compartment door opened. A man in uniform came in and said: "Tickets, please!"

30

The Ticket Collector

An icy thrill went through Tony. With trembling fingers, he groped in his jacket pocket where he had put the tickets he had bought after school the Monday before. Luckily there had been enough money for them in his piggy-bank.

"Here," he said, and handed them to the ticket collector, who took them from him with a nod of his head.

I hope everything's all right! prayed Tony.

"So you're going to Upper Bogsbottom?" The ticket collector looked over the top of his glasses, first at Tony, then at the little vampire. The vampire had pulled his hat down over his forehead so that not much of his face was visible.

"Y-yes, I mean, no," stammered Tony. "I mean, we are actually going to Nether Bogsbottom."

"To Nether Bogsbottom? I see," said the ticket collector.

His voice sounded so odd that Tony did not know whether it was one of the usual grown-up jokes or whether he was really suspicious. To his relief, the lady, who was still groping in her handbag, said: "They're going to visit their aunt."

"You know these two then?" asked the ticket collector.

"That's Auntie Gertie," said the vampire huskily.

The ticket collector looked surprised. "I see. You're travelling together?"

"Yes, yes," said the lady absentmindedly, rummaging further through her bag.

"Oh, that's all right then,' said the ticket collector. "I was just wondering what two young lads were doing travelling alone at this time of night."

At that moment, the lady gave a sigh of relief. "Here it is at last!" she said, handing her ticket to the collector. He glanced at it briefly and gave it back to her.

In her embarrassment, she explained, "I'm sorry to have taken so long. I left my glasses at my daughter's."

"Your glasses?" echoed the ticket collector in surprise. "But there they are in your coat pocket!"

With that, he turned to the door. "We'll be at Upper Bogsbottom in ten minutes," he said, shut the door behind him, turned left and disappeared down the corridor.

31

The Wrong Idea

"My glasses? In my coat pocket?" said the lady in disbelief. "Is that true?"

Tony did not answer. He was sure of one thing only: he and the little vampire must disappear before she put them on! She was already feeling in the side pockets of her coat. She certainly would not find them there, but it would not be long before it occurred to her to look in the breast pocket.

"We must fly!" he hissed to the vampire.

"Fly?" The vampire looked unhappily from the door to the window. "Where to?"

"Outside in the corridor. Anywhere – as long as we don't stay here."

"What about my coffin?"

"We'll take it with us, of course."

Their frantic whispers were interrupted by a cry of surprise from the lady. "They are there!" she exclaimed. With a shake of her head, she drew the glasses out of the breast pocket of her coat. "And to think I thought I'd left them at my daughter's!" She took a silk handkerchief from her bag, breathed on the glasses and began to polish them. She peered at Tony with short-sighted eyes and said reproachfully: "And you let me sit here without them – even though you knew just where they were! Instead of helping me, you were making fun of me!"

"We weren't!" Tony had just finished stowing away the pieces of "Catch the Hat" in his carrier bag. "Come on!" he urged the vampire. "Any minute now she'll have finished cleaning them!"

He stood up, and so did the vampire.

"Yes you were!" retorted the lady. "You've been laughing at me! We'll let the old bag go on looking, you thought – she can't see properly!"

"No!" protested Tony, as he lifted the heavy coffin down from the luggage rack with the little vampire's help. "We only noticed your glasses a moment ago." He did not think for a moment that she believed him, but it did mean she was distracted enough not to finish off her frantic polishing and put the glasses on. If only he could keep her talking until they had managed to get the coffin out into the corridor they would be all right. And it looked as if they would manage it, for she went on with her cleaning.

"Only noticed them a moment ago! Huh!" She laughed, but without humour. "You knew all along where they were!"

In the meantime, Tony had got the door open. "You've got the wrong idea about us," he said, trying once more to convince her. "Now!" He nodded to the vampire, and together they lifted the coffin which they had rested on the seat for a moment.

"Oh really? The wrong idea, have I?" Her voice had become more and more irritated. "We'll soon see, once I've got my glasses on again!"

Tony was already out in the corridor with the front half of the coffin. However, the vampire and the back half were still in the compartment. With a feeling of dread and foreboding, Tony turned to see the lady staring in astonishment through her glasses at the little vampire. She opened her mouth to scream – but could only utter a hoarse whisper.

"A vampire! A real vampire …"

Then she sank back on the cushions in a dead faint and stayed there, motionless.

"Is she dead?" asked the vampire.

"No. She's just passed out," replied Tony who had gone very wobbly at the knees. He had often seen people faint on television, but it was quite different when it happened in real life!

"Come on, quick!" he whispered to the vampire, whose rapt gaze was fixed on the lady's white neck, which showed bare where the scarf had fallen to one side. "Or do you want to wait until she wakes up and summons the ticket collector?"

"I'm coming!" said the vampire. However, he did not budge, but stayed looking greedily at the lady's neck. Tony was getting more and more anxious. At any minute someone could come past, either another passenger, or the ticket collector even ...

"If you stay there one minute longer," he said crossly, "you can get yourself to Nether Bogsbottom without my help!"

This threat seemed to work: the vampire looked guilty and embarrassed. "Okay, I'm coming," he said.

32

Let's Scram!

Cautiously, they carried the coffin through the door and even managed to do so without bumping anything. Once in the corridor, Tony, who was also carrying his carrier bag, put down the coffin with a groan and rubbed his aching fingers.

"I'd love to know whether you'd slave away like this for me!" he said through clenched teeth.

"I-I can carry the coffin by myself!" said the vampire quickly. "Just tell me where we're going."

As always when Tony was justifiably grumpy about something, the vampire tried to divert him! But they were in too much of a hurry to discuss it now, so Tony simply said: "Turn right."

Since the ticket collector had gone left, it seemed to him best if they went in the opposite direction to the end carriage, and they could get out from there.

On shaky legs, his eyes riveted on the swaying floor beneath him, the vampire bore his coffin down the corridor. Beads of sweat stood out on his forehead, and his pointed teeth clicked together loudly. Behind the door that Tony held open for him, he put down the coffin with a bump and sat down on it, exhausted.

"Hey, we've got a bit farther to go!" cried Tony with some urgency.

"I don't feel well," groaned the vampire.

"Do you want the ticket collector to find us?"

"No! But everything's spinning in front of my eyes!" The vampire made such a doleful face that Tony felt genuinely sorry for him. "Can't I just sit here for a while?"

"Hmmm." Tony was undecided. They would certainly be safer in the end carriage; on the other hand, it could not be long now till they arrived in Upper Bogsbottom because the train was already slowing down and on either side of the railway line he could see the lighted windows of houses.

"Okay," he agreed, then added, "but don't attract attention to yourself!"

This warning was unnecessary, of course, for the little vampire certainly would not do anything stupid. But it made Tony feel good to show him yet again how dependent he was on Tony for help and that he, Tony, could tell the vampire how to behave. The vampire gave him a dirty look but made no answer.

"Let's hope you feel better once we get to Upper Bogsbottom," said Tony. "I can't carry your coffin by myself!"

"'Course I will!" growled the vampire. "It's just all this swaying and shaking."

And indeed, the sick look on the vampire's face did improve as the train drew into the station. Without any prompting from Tony, he stood up and pushed the coffin to the carriage door.

In the meantime, Tony had opened it and was peering outside. With relief, he discovered that their carriage had come to a halt at the far end of the platform, quite a way from the ticket hall. An elderly gentleman clutching a bunch of flowers was walking up and down in front of it. Opposite them stood a bicycle rack, past which ran a narrow path flanked by thick bushes. They could reach that quickly and fairly safely – that is, if the vampire co-operated and did not leave Tony in the lurch!

Tony turned to him anxiously, but his fear that once more the vampire might have sunk onto his coffin seemed to have been groundless. The vampire had already lifted his end and was only waiting for Tony to take the front.

"All clear?" he whispered huskily.

Tony nodded. "There's a little overgrown path opposite us. We'll be safe there."

When they had reached the bushes, Tony gave a last look behind them. He saw the lady climb slowly down the steps of the train to be greeted enthusiastically by the gentleman with the flowers – and farther along the train, two other women got out and stood on the platform looking around inquiringly. They were wearing green woollen overcoats, Tyrolean hats and walking shoes.

"Oh crikey! Those two!" he groaned. "Let's scram!"

"Which two?" asked the vampire.

"The ladies with the amazing hats," answered Tony grumpily. We just don't have time to get into a long discussion about them, he thought. It was much more important to find out where this path led to, and how they could get to Nether Bogsbottom.

At the beginning of the path, Tony stopped.

"We'll leave the coffin here and take a look around first." He had to speak quite loudly as a train was passing.

"Leave my coffin here unguarded?" The vampire was outraged. "Never! I'll sit here too till you come back."

That suited Tony very well, because he would be much freer on his own. So he said with a grin, "Okay. But just don't draw –"

"– attention to myself. I know, I know," the vampire interrupted him in irritation. "Don't you worry, sir!"

33

On the Way to Nether Bogsbottom

As Tony went farther along the path, he discovered it led to the road as he had guessed it would. What did surprise him was that there was no fence, no gate, not even trampled wire netting. That's the advantage of a village station, he thought happily. He had been afraid they would have to lift the coffin over a high wall or a barbed wire fence, or, worst of all, that they would have had to go out of the main station exit.

The road lay before him, deserted in the lamplight. There were only two cars parked by the station, a black saloon car and a light blue minibus. The road seemed to end at the station, as behind the parking area all was darkness.

At the top of the road Tony saw a large building, The Lexington Arms, as it proclaimed on a brightly lit sign. The pub lay on the corner of a wider road, the main village street, probably. There was also a signpost.

West Batsteeple 8 kilometres, Tony read on the board pointing to the left and under it: Nether Bogsbottom 1 kilometre. Mildwater 18 kilometres, was written on the sign pointing right.

Tony gave a sigh of relief: at least he now knew which direction to go in. And compared to the train journey, the last kilometre to

Nether Bogsbottom would be child's play. A bit exhausting with the heavy coffin, perhaps – but not half so nerve-wracking.

Tony heard the cars at the station start up. He hid behind a tall pine tree. From there he could survey the road without being seen himself. First the black saloon drove past with the elderly man at the wheel. Tony saw Mrs Poyson sitting next to him, her head laid back. The car drove to the junction and turned right. Then came the light blue minibus. A woman was driving it. On one of the rear seats sat the two ladies in Tyrolean hats. Tony watched them turn left in the direction of West Batsteeple.

He waited a minute longer and listened. The muffled sound of voices came over to him from the pub. Somewhere in the distance, a car hooted, and a dog barked from the other side of the railway line. Village night-life! thought Tony. Luckily no one knew that a vampire was coming to visit them! And if all went well, no one would ever know.

Tony turned round and went back down the path. The little vampire was waiting impatiently for him.

"I thought you weren't coming back," he said.

That made Tony grin. "What would you have done without me? Gone in search of the village cemetery?"

The vampire glared at him. "Just give me a hand with my coffin!" he growled, adding with a sidelong glance at Tony's neck, "or would you rather wait till I get hungry?"

"Hungry?" That gave Tony a fright. "But we're almost at Nether Bogsbottom! Just another kilometre. We'll manage that in no time."

"Do you know the way?"

"Yes."

"Okay then. What are we waiting for?"

The vampire took hold of the back end of the coffin, Tony lifted the front and they carried it as far as the road. There Tony looked carefully left and right, then nodded to the vampire.

"All clear!" he whispered.

The door to the pub was open as they went past. Loud music could be heard, but there was no one to be seen. Tony came to a halt in the shadow of one of the cars parked in the pub car park.

"What is it?" hissed the vampire. "Don't you know the way?"

"Yes of course I do. I'm just wondering which side of the road would be safer."

The vampire looked over to the other side of the road. "The other side, of course. There aren't any houses. What's more, we can hide in the bushes if a car comes past."

"It's tough going though, through all that long grass," replied Tony. He would have preferred to stay on this side and walk on the pavement. There was still quite a way to go and his hands were already hurting.

But the vampire's mind was made up. "It's definitely safer over on that side."

"If you say so," said Tony.

They crossed the road and set off in the direction of Nether Bogsbottom.

After a while, Tony said, "I've got to go."

"Go?" inquired the vampire. "Go where? Go and have a rest?"

Tony cleared his throat. "I – er – I've just got to go."

A car was approaching. Quickly they put down the coffin and ducked behind a bush.

"Don't you ever have to?" asked Tony.

"Have to what?"

"Have a – er – pee?"

"Oh that!" At last the vampire had got the point. "That's what you're on about! No, I haven't peed for about a hundred years."

"Really?" Tony was astounded. "Don't vampires have to?"

Rudolph looked at him with a grin. "Were you wondering if Anna had to?"

"What on earth made you think of her?" retorted Tony, feeling himself blush. "I'll just go over there," he added quickly and disappeared behind a tree.

"Hurry up!"

Soon they were on their way again. Tony's hands were burning and his arms and shoulders felt like lead.

"You okay?" asked the vampire.

"Mmmm," said Tony in a strained voice. A little way ahead he could see the sign saying Nether Bogsbottom. He'd just be able to make it to there.

34

Left in the Lurch

Just beyond the signboard, the road forked. Tony read the street names: Moth Street lay straight ahead, Old Street turned off to the right.

"That's the one!" he cried in excitement.

"What?" asked the vampire suspiciously.

"The street we're looking for. Number 13, Old Street – that's where they live!"

Now that the end of their journey was in sight, Tony found new strength. He walked so fast that Rudolph could hardly keep up.

"There's the farm over there!" Tony felt his heart beat faster. "Can you see it? The big barn and stables, and that white house!"

"How do you know it's that house?"

"Because I've been here before."

"Are you sure it's the right one?"

"Positive."

"Then I don't need you any more!" declared the vampire.

Tony stopped still in surprise. "What do you mean?"

"Simple. I can manage the last bit on my own."

"Oh. And what am I supposed to do?"

"You can go home," said the vampire calmly.

For a second, Tony was speechless. Then he cried: "All by myself?"

"Why ever not?" said the vampire in astonishment. "It'll be much safer on the train without me."

"But there isn't another train!"

"There isn't one?"

"No. I've found that out already."

The vampire looked at Tony in amazement. "And just how did you plan to get home?"

"With you! I specially brought the second cloak Anna gave me."

"So you've got the cloak? Well, that's fine then!" The vampire gave a grating laugh. "You don't need a train. You can just fly home!"

"That's all very well for you!" said Tony furiously. "I bring you all the way here, help you carry this coffin –" He suddenly realised that they were still holding the coffin, and he let his end drop onto the grass.

"Hey!" cried the vampire.

"– and now you can't even be bothered to fly back with me!"

"You don't understand," said the vampire with an embarrassed grin. "I've got to" – he hesitated, then finished – "get settled in here."

"Once more, just thinking of yourself!" said Tony bitterly.

"Vampires have to! Anyway, it's not that bad, flying on your own," he said. "I have to every night, even though I'm afraid of the dark."

"How am I supposed to find the way?"

"You can follow the railway line."

"What if someone sees me?"

The vampire waved airily. "Everyone'll be asleep at this hour. No one will see you."

"What if I meet Aunt Dorothy?"

"She'll think you are a vampire and leave you alone."

At that moment, a loud "Baaaah!" came from the stables. A hungry smile spread over the pale face of the vampire, and his pointed teeth winked in the moonlight. "Did you hear that?" he whispered. "A sheep! A nice fat sheep – full of blood!" He picked up the coffin

and turned to go. "See you tomorrow!" he said
– and vanished among the trees.

Tony watched him go. How could he have
been so stupid as to think the vampire would
come home with him? It certainly wasn't the
first time Rudolph had left him in the lurch!
He thought fearfully of the long, lonely flight
home, but there was no alternative: he would
have to do it! He took the vampire cloak out of
the bag and put it on. Then he spread his arms
wide and fluttered away, rather uncertainly –
like a moth which has burnt itself on a lamp.

35

Grounds for Suspicion

"Wake up Tony!"

Tony opened his eyes. He wondered in bewilderment where the sudden light was coming from. Surely he was still flying through the night sky?

"Tony! Hurry up!" It was his mother's voice. "We must have breakfast!"

"Breakfast?" murmured Tony. But he had to fly home, had to follow the railway line ... Tony's bedroom door opened and his mother came in.

"Tony!" she said reproachfully. "We want to leave early, and here you are, still lazing in bed!"

Tony blinked. So he was at home after all!

"Dad's got breakfast ready, the cases are in the car – we're just waiting for you!"

"Okay, coming –" Tony sat up bleary-eyed. All his limbs ached, especially his shoulders and arms. They felt as if he had been doing weight lifting for hours and hours. He groaned softly.

"So, an evening spent watching telly wears you out, does it?" remarked his mother.

"What?"

"We didn't get home till 2 a.m. but we're not half as tired as you."

"What time is it?"

"Half past nine."

"Half past nine," repeated Tony slowly, scratching his head.

"Tell me now: how late did you watch telly till?"

"I didn't watch it at all," was what Tony would have liked to say, quite truthfully. But then he would have had to think up another reason for sleeping so late, and he was far too tired for that! So he simply said: "Till eleven."

"As late as that!" exclaimed his mother crossly. "We told you quite clearly you could only watch until ten o'clock."

"Are you two coming to breakfast?" called Dad from the kitchen.

"Tony was watching telly till eleven o'clock!" Mum called back. "What do you think of that?"

"I-It was such an interesting programme," said Tony.

"Oh? What was on?"

That gave Tony a fright. He had no idea what programmes had been on the night before!

"I-I've forgotten," he murmured.

"Are you two coming for breakfast or not?" called Tony's father again.

"I'll have a look in the newspaper," announced Tony's mother. "What channel was it on?"

"Er – one."

Tony's mother went out. I hope there wasn't a horror film on yesterday, thought Tony. Otherwise he would be in his parents' bad books for no real reason! He got up and dressed. As he did so, he remembered the vampire's cloak which he had stuffed under the mattress the night before. He absolutely must take it with him to Nether Bogsbottom, but how was he going to manage it? His case had long since been stowed away in the car. It was impossible to wear the cloak. At his wits' end, he looked around his room and his eyes fell on his school satchel lying near his desk – and that gave him an idea.

"Hey, Mum!" he called. "May I take my satchel with me? I've got some work to do for school."

"In the holidays?"

"Yes. It's so I'll be able to get into the selective school."

"Of course you may." Tony thought his mother's voice sounded somewhat distrustful. Up till now, he had never volunteered to take school work away on holiday. And of course she was quite right to be suspicious: the last thing he wanted to do was school work!

He quickly folded up the cloak. He had just hidden it in the satchel under some text books and exercise books when his mother came into the room for the second time. "Are there school books in there?"

Tony forced himself to smile. "Of course."

"Can I see?"

"Why?"

"Because I have a suspicion that you want to smuggle those dreadful vampire books with you to Nether Bogsbottom."

131

"But, Mum –" protested Tony.

"I'm afraid I do. And we can't have that, Tony, you know."

Tony thought for a moment. If she was quite determined to look in the satchel, there was nothing he could do about it. Perhaps he would be lucky and she would not notice the cloak. So with an uneasy feeling, he handed it over.

She pulled out a couple of books and read the titles. Then she shook her head in disbelief. "All school books!" she said to herself. "Then I've done you an injustice."

Tony grinned happily.

"But your satchel doesn't half smell!" she added, puzzled. "So mouldy!"

Tony bit his lip to try not to laugh. "Do you think so?" He quickly buckled up the satchel once more.

"Anyway," remarked his mother, "I'm still amazed at your taste in television programmes."

"What do you mean?"

"Saturday: 8.15 p.m. Opera Highlights; 10.10 p.m. Today's News; 10.15–11.05 p.m. Country Music," she read from the newspaper's television guide.

Tony felt himself go red. "I felt like listening to music," he mumbled in embarrassment.

"To opera and country music? That's a change from usual!"

"Well yes." Tony cleared his throat. "Dad says you should try everything once."

"I also say that the eggs and coffee will be cold unless you two come at once!" It was his father once more calling from the kitchen.

"Coming right now!" answered Mum. She went out. Tony followed, happy to have come through her interrogation!

133

36

Country Air Makes You Tired

Tony tried to read a comic during the drive to Nether Bogsbottom, but soon the letters began to swim in front of his eyes.

"Tony's going to sleep again," remarked his mother, who was driving, and could therefore see him in the driver's mirror.

"That's what country air does for you!" said Dad, who was studying the map of Nether Bogsbottom and its outlying district.

Tony had to bite back a laugh: they had hardly come a quarter of an hour away from home, and already the so-called "country air" was supposed to have made him sleepy! On the other hand, it might well prove a handy excuse during the next few days!

"Yes, that's right," he said. "Country air does make you tired." He yawned broadly to add weight to his words.

"I think it's more likely to be opera highlights and country music!" said his mother sarcastically.

Tony did not deign to answer. Instead, he read a couple more pages from his comic. Then his eyes closed and he fell asleep.

It was night time. Tony was sitting on the branch of a great tree, having a little rest before flying off. The railway line glinted in the moonlight. Everything was calm and still.

Tony leaned his head back against the trunk and closed his eyes for a moment.

Suddenly a loud "Hic!" brought him up with a start. He stared around him in a fright. Had something moved down there on the railway line? He realised it must have been a rabbit, for it disappeared into the undergrowth. Then something else rustled, over by the birch trees. Tony's heart began to beat faster. There was someone down there! Once more it gave a "Hic!" and then a figure in a long black cloak slid out of the shadows of the trees. In the moonlight Tony recognised Aunt Dorothy!

An icy shudder went through him. Had she smelt him out? But Aunt Dorothy seemed to have other things on her mind. She walked with strangely unsteady steps and gave several more "Hics!" looking round her uncertainly. Tony heard her muttering.

"You shtupid d-drunken twit! It'sh all your fault that I've g-got to walk – Hic!" Her voice sounded oddly slurred.

Then Tony suddenly realised why she was behaving in such a peculiar way: she had gone to the village dance – not to dance, of course, but to wait for her prey outside the village hall. It seemed she had chosen a man who had drunk too much – so much that now she could not even fly! And that made Tony smile.

He was still smiling when the car drew to a halt.

"Tony!" It was his father's voice.

Tony looked around him sleepily. "Where are we?"

"In Nether Bogsbottom."

Tony recognised the white house and large barn. And he had also seen the pale blue minibus before, which was parked in front of the barn – yesterday, at the station in Upper Bogsbottom! So the two ladies in Tyrolean hats were also guests at the farm!

"Oh no!" he groaned.

"What's the matter now?" asked his mother in some irritation.

Tony climbed stiffly out of the car. "Nothing. Everything's fine." With a glance at the barn, he added: "Anyway, I bet you there's a vampire living in there!"

"Oh, of course!" said his mother crossly. "That's all that counts, your vampires!"

"I quite agree!" said Tony, rubbing his hands together in contentment.

Other Titles in this Series:

THE LITTLE VAMPIRE
Angela Sommer-Bodenburg
ISBN 0 590 70132 0   £1.25

Tony loves stories about vampires but when the real thing lands on his window-sill one evening and introduces himself as Rudolph, he is not so enthusiastic!

THE LITTLE VAMPIRE MOVES IN
Angela Sommer-Bodenburg
ISBN 0 590 70298 X   £1.00

When Rudolph, the little vampire, is banished from his home, Tony, his friend, lets him move into the basement – coffin and all! But soon, Tony is at his wits end trying to prevent his parents from finding out about the new tenant downstairs!

Coming soon:

THE LITTLE VAMPIRE ON THE FARM
Angela Sommer-Bodenburg
ISBN 0 590 70443 5   £1.25 approx.

Tony's problems were over – he had safely sneaked the little vampire to the holiday home at Nether Bogsbottom! But vampires live in coffins – and where do you hide one of those on a farm?

And another title you will enjoy:

CRY VAMPIRE!
Terrance Dicks
ISBN 0 590 70405 2   £1.25

Anna Markos had disappeared. The police had started a big hunt – but Simon and Sally knew they wouldn't find the young girl. They knew exactly where she was. But what could they do? Who on earth would believe them if they said she'd fallen into the clutches of vampires . . .?